Warlands

Once upon a time, quite a long time ago, in a beautiful faraway city where scarlet-flowering trees grew along wide streets, and where tropical sunsets reddened the evening skies, a small child was lying in the gutter . . .

When Amy goes to stay with her grandmother, she begs her to tell her stories about how Uncle Ho came to live with the family. Ho was a Vietnamese orphan, born amongst the bombings and terror of war, and the nightmares in his head are always with him.

No one really knows the true story of Ho's early life before he came to the family, but Amy's grandmother tells her the same stories she told Ho because, as her granny says, 'everyone needs to know the story of their life, even if it has to be invented.' And although the stories, like all good stories, start with 'Once upon a time,' Amy has to wait to find out if they will end with 'And they all lived happily ever after' . . .

RACHEL ANDERSON was born in 1943 at Hampton Court. She and her husband, who teaches drama, have a daughter and three sons. She has worked in radio and newspaper journalism and in 1991 won the Medical Journalist's Association Award. She has written four books for adults, though now writes mostly for children. She won the Guardian Children's Fiction Award in 1992 for *Paper Faces*. When not writing she is involved with the needs and care of children who are socially and mentally challenged.

Warlands

Warlands

Rachel Anderson

OXFORD
UNIVERSITY PRESS

OXFORD
UNIVERSITY PRESS

Great Clarendon Street, Oxford OX2 6DP

Oxford University Press is a department of the University of Oxford.
It furthers the University's objective of excellence in research, scholarship,
and education by publishing worldwide in

Oxford New York

Athens Auckland Bangkok Bogotá Buenos Aires Calcutta
Cape Town Chennai Dar es Salaam Delhi Florence Hong Kong Istanbul
Karachi Kuala Lumpur Madrid Melbourne Mexico City Mumbai
Nairobi Paris São Paulo Singapore Taipei Tokyo Toronto Warsaw
and associated companies in Berlin Ibadan

Oxford is a registered trade mark of Oxford University Press
in the UK and in certain other countries

British Library Cataloguing in Publication Data available

ISBN 0 19 271817 7

Typeset by AFS Image Setters Ltd, Glasgow
Printed in Great Britain

For my grandsons
Nguyen Edward Robertson and
Merlin Storie Robertson

Everybody needs to know the story of their life, even if it has to be invented.

Amy

Once upon a time, not so long ago, a girl was staying with her grandmother during half-term. She was watching television. Then the news came on.

'Nearly bedtime, Amy,' called the grandmother.

'Granny, what are all those people doing?' the girl asked. On the screen she saw men and women shuffling and scrabbling to climb up onto a truck. She saw armed soldiers pushing them. She saw children crying. She saw a baby sitting by the dusty road alone, not doing anything.

'They're refugees from the war.'

'What's happening to them?'

'They're being taken to a place of safety.'

'I saw a baby. It was on its own.'

'Poor wee mite. It's probably been orphaned.'

'What's that?'

'It means when both parents are dead, so there's no one to take care of it.'

Amy thought that sounded rather exciting, to be alone in the world with nobody telling you what to do.

Her grandmother said, 'Like your Uncle Ho. He was an orphan.'

'But *he's* not a child!' said Amy indignantly. 'He's a grown-up. And he's not on his own. He's got you and Grandad.'

1

Although Uncle Ho was a man, he still needed quite a lot of looking after, sometimes more than Amy.

Her grandmother said, 'Yes, but Ho didn't always have us. There was a time when he had no one.'

Amy said, 'So what'll happen to that baby on the telly?'

'I expect someone will come and get him.'

'Like you got Uncle Ho?'

'Perhaps.'

The news ended. Another programme started.

'Come along now, Amy. Upstairs.'

When she was tucked up in bed, Amy remembered the war-baby on the telly and felt a very tiny bit sad for it, though not so sad that she didn't want a bedtime story. She asked her grandmother to tell her one of her special long-ago stories.

'And which ones are those?' asked her grandmother.

'Like you said you used to tell Uncle Ho when he screamed and screamed all through the night.'

'That was such a long time ago, my dear. I'm not sure I can remember them.'

'Oh, Granny. Please try.'

'Very well, dear. Which one did you want?'

'All of them. From the very beginning until you get to the end.'

'But that would take us from now till breakfast time,' said the grandmother. 'And besides, I'm not sure if there is an end yet.'

'Why isn't there?'

'Because Uncle Ho is alive and well and sitting downstairs, that's why. As you know very well.'

'All right then. Just tell me the first one. I love that one. How they found him in the gutter.' It was such a peculiar place to be found. Nobody with any sense would allow themselves to get put in a filthy gutter.

2

'Very well, Amy. But then you must promise, promise to go straight to sleep and no nonsense.'

''Course I will. I always do when I'm staying with you, because you're the best grandmother there ever was.' Amy sometimes told her other grandmother the same thing because she liked to keep her bread buttered on both sides.

In a Faraway Place

Once upon a time, quite a long time ago, in a beautiful faraway city where scarlet-flowering trees grew along the wide streets, and where tropical sunsets reddened the evening skies, a small child was lying in a gutter. It was late. Most people had long since hurried home and closed their shutters to be safe from raids and thieves and army patrols.

One tired policeman cycled slowly through the fruit market towards his home. He was off duty. All day he had been directing traffic and keeping an eye out for pickpockets.

As he pedalled along the boulevard beneath the flowering flame trees, he heard a frail squeaking sound. He thought it was his bike. He stopped to check the wheels. But the noise continued.

'Meeeew, meeeew.'

The policeman said to himself, 'Hmm, that's funny. It sounds a bit like a newborn kitten.'

He glanced round. He saw, lying on the ground in amongst a pile of market rubbish, a baby. It had huge brown eyes, and a mass of black hair sprouting upwards like spiky bamboo shoots.

The policeman bent down for a closer look. The baby was naked, dirty, and so thin its ribs showed under its skin like little twigs. It was a boy.

3

'Meeew, meeew,' the baby went, though there were no tears when it cried.

When the policeman picked it up, it wasn't heavy for it was little more than a bundle of skin and bones. He searched the nearby streets for someone to hand it back to. But there was no one.

In those days, in that faraway country, finding an abandoned child in the street was not unusual, for there was a war which had been going on for years and years, ever since the policeman had been a schoolboy. Sometimes, children's parents were killed, sometimes they went off into the forests to join the fighting, sometimes they simply ran away from their children because they had no more food and no more love to give them.

Babies were sometimes left with a scrap of paper giving their name. This one had nothing, not even a scrap of cloth for a nappy.

When the policeman found no one to pass the child on to, he heaped up some of the dry rubbish into a comfy nest and he replaced the baby on the pavement. The baby blinked its big brown eyes. It waved its thin scraggy arms and twitched its scrappy little legs.

The policeman said to himself, 'I must get home to my own little boys. My wife will start wondering where I am if I'm late. She'll be so worried. She'll think I've been stopped at a roadblock or trapped by the curfew.'

But as he pedalled away, he could hear the baby's frail mewing following him down the road.

He slowed down. He stopped.

No, no, no, he thought. I cannot leave that baby there, even if it does look as ugly as a skinned rat.

So he turned back and gathered it up out of the rubbish.

4

'Upon the souls of my ancestors, I do not know what I am to do with you now,' he said, holding it uncertainly. 'However, since it was your Fate that you should be left lying in the gutter, and it was my Fate that I should be the one to find you, then it is Fate that will resolve the outcome.'

And, even though the baby was dirty and damp with pee, he tucked it inside the front of his uniform jacket. 'But I really cannot take you home with me. I've five hungry children of my own.'

Because of the war, there were many shortages. There was hardly enough food for the policeman's own sons, his wife, his mother, and his mother-in-law, let alone for an extra one, however small it was.

Just then came the screaming of jets flying in low over the city. You could hear them from a long way off.

EEEEEEeeeeeeeeeeeeee.

They were going to bomb the villages hidden in the deep green forests beyond the city. When they hit a target, there was another sound, bom bom bom, and the ground shook.

Some people said you grew used to it. But the policeman didn't think that the sound of people and homes being smashed was something you ever got used to.

He ran with the baby to one of the round concrete drains that were used as shelters. Sometimes bombs fell short of their targets and hit the city instead. He crouched in the drain until the raid was over and it was safe to hurry home. But the policeman couldn't go to his home yet. He still had the mewing infant tucked in the front of his jacket.

He walked slowly through the deserted market place, pushing his bike with one hand, supporting the baby with the other, wishing he could get rid of it to someone else. But these days everybody had troubles enough of their own.

He came to a broken-down building. It had a roughly painted sign propped on the tin roof which said *Hoi Duc Anh*. Although he went past here nearly every day, he'd never before given it a second thought. *Hoi Duc Anh* meant *The Association for the Protection of Infants*. It was a place where children who had got no one to look after them could stay.

Why, of course! thought the policeman. It is Fate that I have come this way.

The orphanage had once been used as a school. A grumpy-looking old woman was about to secure the main gate for the night with a padlock and chain.

'Yes?' she said sharply. 'What is it?'

The policeman took the dirty child from his jacket and held it out for her. 'I found this,' he said. 'Near the fruit market. Just beyond the fish market.'

'Name?'

The policeman shrugged. 'I have no idea.'

'Then you should have looked for its parents.'

'I did. There was no one.'

'Well, you people can't expect to hand in every abandoned baby you find, just like that. We've got more than enough as it is. Can't you hear them?'

Indeed the policeman could. The distant wailing and grizzling and greeting and crying of a hundred or more sad babies' voices was almost worse than the screaming of an air-raid.

He said, 'I really must be on my way. My wife will be worried.'

'I'm not interested in all that,' said the woman. 'I've got more than enough worries here. If citizens bring in lost babies, I have to follow the proper procedure. Your name, and your address, if you please. I'll fetch the

6

book.' She unlocked the gate and beckoned him into the compound.

'*My* name? Why mine?'

'We have to make sure he's really a stray, and not one of your own that you can't be bothered with. People do that. Then, as soon as we've fattened them up, they reclaim them.'

She left the policeman standing on the verandah of the orphanage while she went off to find her registration book. He waited. And waited.

What am I to do now? the policeman wondered. I really can't stay here all night, and then wait some more while she asks me questions about my name and address. And if I do give her my address, she may hold me responsible for this orphan boy's future welfare. All I need is to be sure that he has a safe place to sleep tonight. I won't wait around another moment for that woman.

So he laid the baby in a big broken wicker chair in the corner by the door where the woman could not fail to notice him when she returned.

'I have done the best that I can,' said the policeman to himself as he climbed onto his bike and pedalled away. 'At least the boy will now sleep with a roof over his head.'

In fact, the rusty tin roof of the orphanage had holes in it that let in the rain. And there were many fat happy rats that lived in the rafters. But the policeman was not to know that.

The baby lying in the wicker chair put his fist into his mouth and began to gnaw and mew at the same time.

When the woman came back with her big book, she was irritated to find the man had gone.

'Oh my, what a to-do. Where's the fellow that brought you in? This is absurd, just dumping you here.

7

It really won't do. But that's what they all do these days. No civic responsibility.'

The baby stared without seeing. He was now so tired and so hungry that he couldn't even be bothered to make the squeaky mewing noise.

'Oh, all right then, you,' the woman grumbled, and she picked him up, not very gently. 'You can stay. But just look at the sight of you, no clothes, covered in scabs, scraggy as a wet dog. *And* you've piddled all over the chair!'

She carried him to a bleak room, more like a shed, where there were a hundred and more children and babies. Fifty smaller ones lay down one side of the room on newspaper and blankets. Fifty-three older ones were contained in wire cots down the other side.

What a din and what a smell there was in that place. But at least there was a roof over everybody's heads and a chance of being fed. The orphanage had cartons of powdered milk and feeding bottles, though not enough of either to go round one hundred and three people. Each child had its brief turn. When their time was up, the dribbling teat was pulled from their lips and thrust into the next mouth in the line.

The grumpy woman wrapped a piece of torn cotton cloth round the latest arrival and laid him on the newspaper with the others to wait for his turn.

The next morning, in the office of the orphanage, the woman opened up the big book to fill in the details.

'We got a new boy handed in last evening,' she told one of the younger women who came to help at the *Hoi Duc Anh*. 'Picked up by a traffic policeman. The child looked near death last night. Didn't think he'd be alive by morning. But he's hanging on. If he lives, he'll have to have a name.'

8

The younger woman said, 'Could we call him Ho?'
Her brother was called Ho. He was sixteen. He was a
soldier away fighting. The young woman hadn't seen
him for months. She wasn't even sure if she ever would
see him again.

'Very well,' said the older woman. 'That's certainly
better than calling him Boy-Baby.' There were already
two children whose only name was Boy-Baby. 'And
we'll need family names too.'

Even though the latest arrival didn't seem to have a
family, he still needed a family name in order that the
book could be properly filled in. Even a makeshift
wartime orphanage had to keep its accounts in order.

The younger woman said the first name that came into
her head. 'What about Ly Thanh?' It had been her last
schoolteacher's name.

'Very well,' said the older woman. With a sigh, she
wrote down that the unknown child's name was: *Ly
Thanh Ho*, that he was male, that his former address
was: *The Central Fish Market*. 'And now we're supposed
to fill in his age. Though I really don't know why I'm
bothering with all this. He's almost certainly going to
die during the next bout of measles.'

The younger woman, who was more hopeful, said,
'Well, how old did he seem?'

The older woman shrugged. 'I saw he's got teeth so
he's clearly not newborn. But he's very small, can't sit
or hold his head up. Perhaps he's about one? Or maybe
one and a half? Or maybe two?'

'Who knows anything about any of these children?'

The book had to be filled in so the woman wrote
down that the boy was aged one and a half years. But
she was tired of making things up just for the sake of
keeping the accounts book up to date in case one of the
city administrator's came to check up. So, where she had

9

to note *Father's Name* and *Mother's Name*, she wrote the truth.

Parents: Unknown.

Then both women went off to start mixing up the powdered milk. To be on the safe side, they added an extra bucketful of water to make it go further for nobody knew when the next delivery might arrive.

Later, the younger woman crept back into the office, opened up the registration book and, under *Ly Thanh Ho*, she changed his address from *The Central Fish Market* to *The Central Flower Market* because, as everybody in every country of the world knows, flowers smell far sweeter than fish.

So now, the brown-eyed boy, sleeping in the big bleak room with the noise of grizzling and whimpering all around him, had a name, an age, and a former address of his very own, even if he didn't have anything else.

When he woke again, the boy now called Ly Thanh Ho felt wet, hungry, and unsure where he was. He began to cry, along with the others around him. He cried intermittently until mid-day when another plastic feeding bottle, half full of pale watery milk, was pushed into his mouth.

By the end of the week, Ly Thanh Ho had learned that if ever a feeding bottle came near, he must suck as fast as he could because it would not be his for long.

And so, Ly Thanh Ho remained exactly where he was with the Association for the Protection of Infants for one thousand, four hundred and fifty-six days, which was four years, until Fate decreed that it was time for something else to happen to him.

Amy

Most holidays, she came to her grandparents. Amy liked the way everything in their house stayed the same and was nicely old-fashioned. Even the toys she played with, the wooden domino bricks, the split cricket bat and worn stumps, the dented metal cars and road signs, had a feel of the olden days about them.

'Don't lick your fingers, dear, not after you've been touching those little cars,' her grandmother warned. 'They're made of lead. It's poison.'

'Gives you brain damage,' her grandfather said with a chuckle.

'Really?' said Amy. She never could tell with him when he was telling the truth.

'Yes, really. That's why they don't make toys out of lead any more.'

Amy knew these were the same things that her dad, her Uncles Ben and Ho, and her Auntie Josie had played with when they were young. She sometimes came across their names written in one of the dog-eared picture books. It was a comforting feeling to know that where she now played, her own father had once played.

At night, lying safe and snug in the cosy little bed, she asked her grandmother, 'That story you told me last night, was that *really* what happened to my Uncle Ho?'

It seemed so different from the unchanging way her grandparents and her Uncle Ho now lived.

'We don't know, dear,' her grandmother replied. 'But it certainly might have, mightn't it? And even if it didn't happen to him, it happened to plenty of others like him. That war went on, day after day, week after week till people in every corner of the world had heard about it.'

Amy said, 'But, Gran, if so many people knew, and if so many people were getting hurt, why didn't someone try to stop it?'

'Because, my dear, there are plenty of folk for whom war is a jolly fine thing. It makes them get rich. It gives them something to do. They're usually men. They're like dogs. Dogs love a good fight, even if it's somebody else's.'

Amy didn't believe her grandmother but when she started to say so her grandmother said firmly, 'Now it's time for sleeping, Amy dear, not talking. Perhaps, another day, another story.'

So Amy, snug beneath the soft quilt, lay down as quiet and good as the innocent and treasured little lamb that she was who knew nothing of the slaughterhouse fate that awaits other less fortunate lambkins.

The Tale of the Dogs of War
as Told by Dingo

Once upon a time, quite a while ago, in a pleasant yet dull suburban street not far from here, there lived a young pup who was bored out of his head.

'You're little better than a mongrel,' his mother used to say when he was a wee tot. Every time she looked at him lying on her bed she wondered what to do with him. He was semi-orphaned; that is to say, he'd been sired by an unknown male of no fixed abode who'd long since bounded away into the night, the sneaky cur. So his son never knew him.

His mother, whom the neighbours all termed a bitch, nursed her no-pedigree pup for as long as she could. She thought she loved him. But how could she be sure?

He was small and runt-like. She was poor and hungry. Soon, she hadn't enough milk to feed him. One bitter cold night, her milk and the tenpenny piece in the gas meter both ran out at the same moment. Now, she had neither nourishment nor warmth to offer her pup. So she picked him up by the scruff of his neck and carried him to the steps of the Town Hall.

And she dumped him.

'There you go, kiddo,' she said, patting him farewell. 'You'll be better off here. Provided you make it through the night. Thank the Lord there's only the one of you. If I'd had a big litter, I'd have found it hard to let them all go. But given there's only the one of you, it's better this way. You go your way. I'll go mine.'

She dragged some torn sheets of newspaper over from the rubbish dump to cover him with.

'You'll do well, my son, I know it. There's something in your eyes that tells me you'll look out for yourself. Just hang on and, come morning, them inside the Town Hall, they'll find a nice respectable family for you.'

She was right on that. The clerks inside the Town Hall found him a nice new home.

And I lived there, for this is my own tale that I am telling, I don't need no help from any hired storyteller, and was fed and educated for several skull-scrapingly boring years. And dog years, I assure you, are as bad as dog-days. They last lo-o-o-o-ng.

Nice enough folks. Two old biddies, into their forties, couldn't manage a litter of their own. They named me

13

Darren. They said I responded well to fair treatment. But was I bored in their respectable company? Bored out of my frisky young scalp. Done my school work. Not too good, not too bad. Just right to be invisible. Stay in the middle stream. Keep your head down, that was my motto. Lie doggo so nobody notices you're there till you're ripe and ready to fend for yourself. And then I'd be off, just like my doggy-dad before me, to seek out the B-side of life.

'You're working for your future, lad,' says the old man who was my pretend dad, patting me on the shoulder. 'Got to keep at it. Nose to the grindstone. Sink or swim.'

Working for my future? What future's that? If I wait around till the future, I'll be an old hound with a grizzly muzzle. It's *now* that I need a taste of the good life.

'Listen, lad,' the old man pleads with me. 'Give education a try. You're young yet. You don't see things same as I do.'

He's not even my real dad. He's only a Town Hall dad. He's been good to me. But that's not enough.

At school, they sense trouble. The Arts and Crafts teacher takes me aside with a smarmy smile. He tells me personal and special, 'It's important, Darryl—'

'Darren,' I say.

'Yes, that's it. Darren. Don't mess it up. It's important for all kids to stick with their school work. But specially for the likes of you.'

I know what he means. Like you who've come up from the gutter, out of nowhere, wrapped in a shred of newspaper without any past to call your own. Don't know your own father. Haven't seen your mother since she dumped you on the steps of the Town Hall. Haven't even got a proper name to yourself. Darren Dog.

14

'Stick with it,' kindly teacher tells me. 'And you'll be OK. You've got that look in your eye, lad. You're going to go far.'

He's said it. Going to go far. So the sooner I begin my travels the better.

That evening after school, after the six o'clock news when they showed those big American bomber planes cruising so smooth and elegant over the green jungles and letting drop their magic cargo, POW!, I went upstairs and I packed my kitbag. I came downstairs. The news was over. Time for *Coronation Street*.

'Ma,' I said. She wasn't even my real ma, but she'd been a good biddy to me ever since she picked me out from the others at the Town Hall dog-pound. So I wasn't going to sneak out without telling her. 'Ma, I'm off to seek my fortune, like my first mother always told me to.'

'Oh, son,' she said, with tears in her eyes, but not grabbing me like you might expect a real mother to, not hugging so close you couldn't breathe and would decide not to go after all. Not causing any hassle. So I could tell she was never my real mother.

'Oh, son, yes,' she said, like she always knew I'd be going sooner or later. 'You got that look in your eye. You always had it.'

She went to the dresser. She took the little key off the hook. She pulled open the drawer. She unlocked the little tin box. She took out the blue fiver and she give it me. And I take it careful, just like I never knew all along it was waiting there in the tin box in the drawer. I take it like I didn't know it was there, like I never had my eye on it all along. The fact she gave it me with her own hand, made me glad I never took it earlier when she was pegging out the sheets. She washes my sheets every morning. I wet them every night. I always have. I don't

15

know why. I just do. But that's no reason not to go and seek your fortune, just because you wet the bed at night. Maybe if I don't have a bed to sleep in, I won't go wetting it.

'Here you go, Darren lad,' she says.

'Thanks, Ma.' Even though she's never my real ma. No more than Darren's my real name. So I changed it there and then to Dingo which is a kind of a dog.

'D'you know where you're going then?' she says, holding on to my hand with the fiver in it just a second too long. 'No, son, no, I ought never to have asked. Why, you probably don't even know yet yourself, do you? You young scallywag!'

Know where I'm going? 'Course I know. I've heard it on the radio. I've read it in the paper. I've seen it every flipping night on the goggle-box.

I am going to cross the seas, and travel halfway round the world to the far side. I am off to watch the Yanks trash the gooks.

And I'm taking my little camera with me and I'm going to snap! snap! snap! all I see, of the soldiers slaying one another deep in green jungle. I'm going to send those pics back to the newspapers and I'm going to make so much money I won't know what to do with it and I'm going to have me some wild fun at the greatest war party there ever was.

In that fabled faraway land, where even the trees in the streets flowered red like flames of fire, and where the girls wore blossoms in their glossy hair, I came alive.

Here was the best war of all time. Everybody was there. The city was crowded with famous faces. I recognized the film stars. I saw the jazz players, dancers,

16

and singers flown in to entertain the troops. World-class writers gathered to get inspiration from watching some of the finest bravest fighters, on both sides, killing each other with every means known, with rocks and stones, with spears and sharpened sticks, with bamboo staves, with traps, with magic fiery chemicals, with millions of tons of TNT.

'Anyone missing out on this is a fool,' a stranger in a bar told me. 'This war is the start of modern history.'

I was hooked from that first night. Streaks of tracer fire went arcing through the sky like meteorites. The giant rumble underfoot of heavy pounding in the far distance, the heady sniff of gasoline. The throbbing hum of choppers. It was pure magic.

In the market, I got myself a tin water bottle, a pair of drab green jungle fatigues, with pockets down the legs to carry my rolls of film. I hitched myself up with a platoon. They let me go with them on their Seek and Destroy.

Dipping and bobbing over the green treetops, then down into a clearing. Jump down from the hovering chopper. They trot along, single file, Indian style. I follow carefully in the steps of the lieutenant. He's the point-man right now, the leader of the line. He says he knows the mines like the back of his hand. Where he steps, I step, like we're playing follow-my-leader in the playground, except these aren't schoolkids. They're men. Then the big guy out front freezes. I freeze. The guy behind freezes. His big boots stay glued to the ground. I stay still. The front guy turns his head. He beckons.

'Whassat?' I say.

I think he's beckoning to me. I think he's showing me something I should snap.

Heck no. He's beckoning to our native guide.

'Come forward, upfront, kiddo!' he orders.

Lieutenant wants the local guy to be point-man, to go first.

Nice move. Put him up there. It's his country. Let him step on the mines.

'Heck, man,' says lieutenant. 'It's his pesky jungle. His pesky brothers laid these mines. I ain't risking my neck for a frisking peasant. I never liked these people. They'll never give nothing away, never trust you.'

So the little brown guy walks out front. Cautiously. No one wants to be point-man. No one wants to be killed first.

We came out of that one alive. I got my pics. Thatch huts burning. Villagers running. Newspaper editor back home pleased. Sends money, more rolls of film. I take more pictures. War and killing and blood and flesh with a background of exotic Eastern beauty, that's what the newspaper public are after.

I get a Press pass. I can go where I like. It's my own risk, just so long as I keep taking pictures, sending them off. Got to keep the folks back home happy. When I've taken enough for the week, I hitch a ride out of the fighting, and buy myself a nice cool beer and sit on the hotel verandah and watch the pretty girls go by, and the pretty sunsets against the waving palm trees.

I didn't do it just for the money. It was comradeship. Those grunts, I loved them. They became the band of brothers I always wanted. At last, I wasn't alone. I was one of the litter, even if I was still the runt.

Then one time, it seemed no different from any other patrol, I'm out with them in the jungle, tiptoeing dainty as a pixie, Indian file. The point-man out front steps. Then the lieutenant steps. Then another guy ahead of me. One two three step. Pause. Step. And suddenly, it's Whooma Sploosha Banga for the fellow in front. Fifteen minutes ago, I was talking to him on the chopper. Now, everything gone. Picked off by a sniper. Just a heap of tattered fatigues lying in the dirt.

So what? The first time it happens, you force yourself to hold it in, to stop yourself howling like a lost dog, so you'll seem like a grown man. And after a while this holding back and holding in becomes real. The feelings don't happen any more. You're tough and hard and mean as a dingo right through.

When your friends get killed right in front of your eyes, you just have to make new friends. In war, that's easy.

But back in the city, there's a new mood. Something uneasy hanging in the air like a bad smell. And the world beyond our little corner of tropical splendour is growing frustrated. That's bad for me. The editor wants new angles.

'Animals!' he telexes me. 'Animals at work in war!'

'Yes, sir.'

So I snap Asian geese guarding bridges, Yankee sniffer dogs searching out explosives, mad-eyed Alsatians guarding PX stores, Indian elephants carrying loads so heavy that even the little local guys on their pedal bikes couldn't shift them.

There's more trouble ahead. The warring enemies are trying to sort out a ceasefire agreement. They're off to Paris, France. They're gathered at a round table. There's talk of a signed treaty.

I sit in my usual place beside the wide boulevard, watch the people pass, see the pretty flowers, drink my beer.

'Heck,' I say. 'There it goes, my easy-win pay-packet. Another war done. Have to go find me a new war.'

But it's going to be OK. The ceasefire wasn't worth the paper it was signed on. The guys out in the jungle didn't get to hear about it. They just keep on lobbing their hand grenades at each other to carry on with the killing.

19

Amy, safe in her quiet bed

'Granny,' said a little girl. 'I don't like this story.'

'No, Amy dear,' said the old lady. 'You're quite right. It's not a nice story at all. I should never have started telling it. I won't tell any more. I'll stop there and you must go to sleep.'

But could a girl sleep when she'd been hearing such a horrid tale?

'Granny, I'm not sleepy yet,' said Amy.

'Very well, dear. I'll tell you a lovely story about the pixies having a picnic tea in a woodland glade.'

'Please, Granny. Won't you go on with the other story? I don't like it. But I have to hear what happens to Ho.'

'Nothing happens to Ho,' said the grandmother. 'Nothing at all. That's the point.'

'Please tell it anyway,' said Amy.

'Very well. Meanwhile, over the other side of the city, in the Hoi Duc Anh orphanage, time passed. Seconds, and minutes, days and weeks, months and years. A boy lived in his wooden crib with no mattress. No bombs fell on him. No one visited him. Ly Thanh Ho lay and whimpered. He got sick. He recovered. He got covered in green boils all over his head. They shaved his scalp. The boils got better. He got sick again. He howled. He heard sounds in the night. And he got frightened.

But he wasn't anyone special. The same thing was

happening to the other children. Some of them died. Some of them survived. Life is a chancy game.

And the war went on. And the bombings were coming nearer to the city. Some nights no one could sleep for the noise and the fear. Some nights wounded soldiers came in and stole the children's sheets for bandages. Most nights rats came down from the rafters and stole the children's rice.'

Dingo

The war was tough on children. But times were hard for everybody, even for Dingo, the world-famous teenage photographer. I was getting wiped out. I'd had enough of legs off and heads blown in. I was bored with corpses and choppers shooting out flames. If they didn't make *me* wince any more, they'd not make the readers wince. I'd seen men in pain. But soldiers know what they're here for. I wanted something new. I needed the thrill of a new kind of suffering, of soft people, women and kids.

I heard they'd begun airlifting orphan kids out of the country and back to the United States, the cute smiling popsies that some of the US Army personnel had taken a fancy to. What a great souvenir to take home to the wife.

'Look, honey, I brought you a little baby girl to bring up. To appease my own conscience for what I done to her country.'

But I'm not keen on kids. So I didn't go along to the airbase to watch the send-off. And all because I hate kids I missed out on a truly great picture opportunity. They had a big transport plane named Galaxy, like the pretty stars in the Milky Way. It's loaded high with smiling kids, all leaving for the land of opportunity. There's a great send-off.

Bye-bye babies.

Straight after take-off, before the people on the ground have even finished waving into the sky, the Galaxy blows up.

Did the fuel tanks catch fire? Did someone shoot it down? Who knows? Who cares? Kids and crew get roasted to a cinder and float down into the South China Sea.

That was some story. My picture editor would have whooped for it. And I missed it all because I can't stand kids.

I had to overcome my dislike. Suffering war orphans are the newest news story. My new bread and butter. So I better find some fast. The barman at the Rex hotel gives me the name of one of the orphanages near where he lives.

'Hoi Duc Anh,' he says. 'You go there, Dingo, you find what you want.'

'The what?' I say. All this time in their country and I still don't know their language. He writes it for me on a piece of paper.

I tip him twenty piastres and I hoof it down to the wrong side of town so's I can get a piece of the action. Suffering kiddies. A market women directs me down a narrow lane running with sewage. Round here, there's fewer flowering trees, more piles of rubbish.

I came to a rough, broken-down building with a tin roof. The gate was secured with a padlock and fat chain. I shouted through a hole in the gate at a woman washing in a trough in the yard.

When she sees the camera slung round my neck, she lets me in and waves me towards the building. Perhaps she thinks I'm someone important, who can make a difference.

I looked in at the kids. I snapped them. Room after room of them. So many living there, if you could call it living. Not going anywhere. Not doing anything. Such a stench. Some rocked themselves from side to side and moaned. Some bit themselves. Most did nothing but lie and stare at the walls. The flies were having a field day, eating the dirt off the children's faces. So few women to take care of so many.

Snap! snap! snap! The editor's going to love this. Though he won't get the smell.

At school, in the days when I went to school, there was a wormery. That's what one of those rooms reminded me of. It was a mass of writhing, wriggling flesh in dirt. Slowly, sluggishly, this way and that, limbs entwined, on blankets on the floor. Some were big, some were small. Some were lolling and dribbling. A writhing mass of miniature humanity with distorted faces, withered limbs, crooked eyes looking two ways at once.

I couldn't believe what I was seeing. They were all of them handicapped. Runts of the litter. Seconds. Rejects. Throw-outs. They should've been put out of their misery ages ago. Snap! snap! My camera will have to tell the merry tale.

I use up all my film. I get out as fast as I can. The woman in the yard clasps my hand in hers and yacks at me in her sing-song way. I think she's trying to thank me.

What for? I'm earning myself some bread and butter. But I'm not here to get involved.

Next time I heard there was to be an airlift, I hoofed it to the airbase as fast as I could. Bluffed my way through the perimeter fence, flashed my Press card at a corporal on the tarmac. I grabbed a small kid off a truck as though I was part of the care team, and held it tight and tender in my arms as though I loved it. And suddenly, there I was striding up the ramp onto that transit plane that's already raring to go.

So then I'm on the airlift. Snap snap out of the porthole, down at the green sea below, the soft silty coastline of the delta. And we don't blow up on take-off.

They've stripped out the insides of the plane. No seats, no carpets, no floors, no walls, to make more space. With the inside linings of the cabin removed, it was so noisy you couldn't hear if the kids were crying, just see their open mouths like goldfish, and so many jammed in together you'd think we'd all suffocate. The babies are in cardboard boxes, miniature paupers' coffins, lined up like they're grocery cartons waiting for dispatch.

The bigger kids that won't fit inside cartons are set in lines on blankets. There must be over a hundred of them. But there's enough women to look after them, Australians, Americans, a few British. I put a new roll of film in my camera. I sized up the nearest bunch of kids, staring, big-eyed. Great picture. I can see it already on tomorrow's front page.

Then I realize they're all like the ones I saw in the upper room at that dumping place, lollers and dribblers. Maybe they're the same ones. Don't all kids look alike? Specially gooks.

I'm with a cargo of cripples. Have I got to photograph handicapped kids?

I said to one of the nurses, 'Why are you bothering with these kiddy crips? Do they have names? Who needs them?'

She smiles and nods nicely. She can't hear above the rattling wings that keep us airborne.

'What are they gonna do with them?' I shout.

She hears me. 'They're being taken to a place of safety,' she shouts back.

24

'What for?'

'To save them.'

'Why?' We have to keep shouting to make ourselves heard.

'Compassion.'

I don't know what she means by that. I shout in her ear, 'Then what?'

She shrugs. 'I dunno.'

'If you ask me, nurse Ozzie, they'd be better off dead.'

But she wasn't asking me.

She was busy with the other nurses giving out drinks of water to the children.

Can you believe it? We're all of us panting with thirst and she gives her water to the crippled kids first, before me, before herself. Kids not worth the space they take up.

Finally, the Australian nurse offers me a little paper cup. I'm fed up waiting. I push it away. In the platoon, the guys always offered refreshment to me first. They used to say, 'Come on, Dingo, you go first. You're our passport to immortality. Take our picture. Go on. Then we'll live for ever.'

The nurse shouts, 'I guess maybe some charity has a plan to try to rebuild their lives.'

'Rebuild? You ever been to UK?'

She hasn't.

'You just haven't a frisking clue then, girl. Britain's no place for rebuilding lives. Nobody wants them there. Using up on resources. There's little enough for Brits. There wasn't anything there for me. They don't need them. They don't want them.'

She was about to reply. But one of the kids begins to throw up. She crawls along the bulkhead floor to hold out a paper bag.

25

'Where's our first stop?' I shout.

'Hong Kong. Refuelling.'

Right, I'm thinking. That's where I get off.

But while I'm still aboard with them at thirty thousand feet, I snap away. My images of this airload of suffering humanity must get to London fast. These are my passport to a fortune. Smile for the camera, there's a good lad.

When I've used up all my film, I feel around in one of my fatigue pockets for a cigarette. I offer one to the nurse. She says no. I blow the smoke into the face of a kid on the floor. If you think of them as worms in a wormery, they're no trouble. He's trying to claw his way towards the shadowy corners of the plane. There's a name-tag on his twiggy wrist.

Ly Thanh Ho, it says.

'Sorry, kiddo,' I say. 'Can't take your piccy. No film left. Better lucky next time.'

The kid stares at me with his deep dark eyes and begins to scream. But you can't hear it. He goes on screaming all the way to Hong Kong. And he won't even stop when the plane lands.

I got off. The cargo flew on to a rapturous welcome in London. I read some of the headlines later.

WAIFS OF WAR JET IN! INNOCENTS SAVED FROM HELLFIRE! ORPHANS PLUCKED FROM DEATH!

Amy's Uncle Ho

'Oh, Granny,' she said sleepily. 'I'm *so* glad Ho got to London all right. And were you and Grandad there to meet him at the airport?'

'No, dear. I'm afraid not. We didn't even know he existed. We were far too busy bringing up our other children.'

'My dad?'

'That's right. And Josie. And Ben. At the time of the airlift, Ben, your Uncle Ben, was still almost a baby. Another little child was the last thing on our minds.'

'So when *did* you get him then?'

'Not for a long time to come. There were hundreds more days to be lived through first.'

Amy's Uncle Ho was a small quiet man with bad teeth. He had black eyebrows and shiny black hair with a few grey streaks in it. He smiled sometimes. But he didn't often speak and even when he did, Amy couldn't always understand him. He was always calm, even when there were small disasters, like Granny catching the frying-pan on fire and burning the sausages to a cinder.

Occasionally, Amy's grandmother sent Uncle Ho and Amy on errands. They walked down to the village store side by side in silence. Uncle Ho had the money and the shopping list which he pushed across the counter to the shop assistant without saying anything.

27

When he'd got the bread, the tea bags, and the tomatoes which Amy's grandmother wanted, he turned to Amy.

'Choct?' he said.

'What?' said Amy.

'Choctty?' he repeated.

'Oh. Right. You mean chocolate,' said Amy. 'Yes, please. Thanks.'

Uncle Ho fished some money out of his other pocket and chose a small bar of milk chocolate. When they were outside the shop, he divided it carefully into two and handed half to Amy.

'Nutty,' he said.

'What?' said Amy.

'Choctty got nutty in.'

It was hazelnut chocolate.

'Yes,' said Amy. 'It's nice. Thank you.'

They walked back together, eating chocolate, in a contented silence. Amy wondered what Uncle Ho thought about the stories of his life, whether he liked them, or even remembered them. They were practically home, already in through the garden gate and going up the path. She decided to seize her chance.

'Uncle Ho,' she began, 'what was it like, I mean really like, to be born in a war?'

Uncle Ho glanced sideways at her. For a moment, Amy thought he hadn't understood what she'd asked. Then he fixed his brown dark eyes on hers. He stared without blinking, almost without seeing her. Amy was afraid. She'd never been afraid of her uncle before. What was he going to do to her? She should *never* have asked anything. She looked away to keep Uncle Ho's eyes from boring into hers.

'It—' he began. 'It—' But whatever it was, he couldn't finish saying it.

28

Instead, he opened wide his mouth which was filled with its gaps and rotten toothy stumps, and out of the dark red depths of his throat came a low howl. It didn't stop. It went on and on like the wailing of a hundred, a thousand, a million crying babies.

Amy's grandmother came scurrying out of the back door.

'Ho!' she said gently. 'Come along now, dear, it's all OK. You know it is.'

But the howl continued and Uncle Ho sank to the floor on his knees, lower and lower as though he were a worm dissolving into liquid.

'Tim!' Amy's grandmother called out to Grandad, more sharply than Amy had ever heard her before. 'Please come now! We need you.'

Grandad came. He was an old man who could scarcely carry in the log basket by himself. Yet suddenly he had ancient strength. He crouched down on the path. He put out his old stiff arms. He gathered up Uncle Ho.

'Come along, old son,' Amy heard him say.

Grandad staggered with Ho to a chair. He held Uncle Ho on his lap with his arms wrapped round him. An old grandad cradled an uncle in his arms.

The howl faded. Amy saw how he whimpered. He trembled on his father's lap. Uncle Ho's melted body was limp. Uncle Ho laid his head on his dad's shoulder. He nuzzled into his old dad's beard. He didn't look like an uncle. He looked like a big grown-up baby. Amy wanted to cry. She went very quietly upstairs to her bed in the attic room. She didn't need a bedtime story.

Later, her grandmother came up to her with a mug of warm cocoa.

'You see, Amy my dear, there are some things Uncle Ho doesn't need to talk about any more. We've talked about them enough in the past. We all know what they are. That's why we have the stories.'

'Yes,' said Amy. 'I'm sorry I've hurt him. I didn't want to hurt him.'

'Of course not, my dear. I'm sure you didn't. Nobody ever *meant* to hurt him. It was just that they didn't always think through the consequences of their actions.'

The Land of Hope and Glory

The season in England was early summer. The weather was shivery. As soon as they arrived at the airport, the children had to be pushed and pulled and shoved into warm clothing.

'Before the wee mites die of pneumonia,' said one of the team of women who'd volunteered to help for the day.

Garments were picked at random from a black plastic bin-bag. The long-sleeved jerseys, the uncomfortable dungarees, the tight nylon socks, felt strange on bodies used to wearing nothing. The wool chaffed their skin and rubbed their necks.

The rescued children had no bits of paper to prove who they were, or who they might once have been. They had only the tags on their wrists, showing names which passing strangers had chosen for them. By leaving their country of origin without identification papers, they had given up their right to a national identity. They didn't belong anywhere. They didn't belong to anybody.

So once they'd been dressed in warm clothing, the refugees (as they were now called) had to be sorted into the good and the bad, the wanted and the unwanted.

The good refugees were the healthiest-looking ones with limbs and minds which appeared to work OK.

They weren't blind, or deaf, or broken in spirit. The good ones were those with bright twinkling eyes. The good ones didn't have boils or scabs all over their scalps.

A crowd of photographers pushed forward across the airport arrivals lounge to get a good look. It was a great story for the newspapers. Starving orphans rescued out of a war-ravaged jungle filled with savages.

The newsmen wanted pictures. Crack! crack! crack! went the flashlights of their cameras. 'Hey! Over here, Mister Big Eyes! Look this way, sonny. Towards me. That's the way. That's what we want. Nice big smile now.'

The good ones could smile a winsome smile.

The bad ones grizzled.

The good ones were the small young ones who might just about pass as babies. People were more willing to take on a baby, specially if it had a bright twinkling smile. They didn't know that a child might be smiling on the outside, but holding dark secrets on the inside.

Ho was one of the leftovers. Ho was too small and scraggy with his bones sticking out like twigs for anyone to choose him. Who'd want a boy with big sad eyes like a wet spaniel staring at them all day? He couldn't walk by himself. He couldn't talk. He peed himself. He pooed himself. He was about six years old. Or seven. Or more. Or less. Nobody cared one way or the other. He was just another speck of alien dust among thousands being lifted into the air, and scattered around the globe in Britain, Germany, Sweden, Australia, Switzerland, Canada, America.

The leftovers were taken that night to an empty Children's Reception Centre until somebody in authority could decide what to do with them.

'These unaccompanied refugee children are always a problem,' said a civil servant irritably. 'We haven't had to cope with this kind of situation for over thirty years.'

This time, some of the government civil servants were already thinking it might be best to send them back to where they'd come from.

'Then at least they won't have a language problem.'

The Children's Reception Centre, at Helmore House, was a large gloomy building standing in large, gloomy, and uncared-for grounds. Inside, it was as cold and draughty as the Hoi Duc Anh had been stiflingly hot. At least there were no rats in the roof, nor weevils in the foodstore. At least there was food each day. It was not rice, rice, rice. But potato, potato, potato. Mashed, boiled, or chipped.

'All children enjoy my lovely crispy chips,' said one of the volunteers who came in to do some cooking. Not these children. They were used to rice.

Apart from getting used to chips and scratchy clothes, not a lot happened. Ho and the other leftovers had exchanged one kind of meaningless existence for another.

The dark shadowy things behind the eyes stayed the same. Inside Ho's head, there were bombing raids, night skirmishes, explosions, and black-outs. These were the things that he'd brought with him, the only possessions that were truly his own.

Even the name given him was no longer his. On the flight, the *Ly Thanh Ho* tag had slipped off his wrist. A young man called Dingo had picked it up. He'd given it to an Australian nurse. She'd tied it to the foot of a baby in a cardboard box. As the plane was landing, she noticed the baby had two tags and a small boy had none. She removed the tag from the baby's wrist and tied it on to Ho's wrist. So Ly Thanh Ho had become the name of a smiling baby who'd caught the eye of an air stewardess.

'I'll take that one,' she'd said. 'Yes, the one in the box.'

The new Ly Thanh Ho was gathered up and driven away in a big car to live in a farmhouse with a pony in a paddock.

And Ho became Phan Thanh Ho.

'Such stupid foreign names they've got,' said one of the voluntary helpers at Helmore House. 'Phan Thanh Ho indeed! Tin Pan Alley more like! How are we supposed to get these names right? They all sound alike and they're next to impossible to pronounce. If they're going to become British, they ought to give them sensible names.'

Ho looked at the mouth speaking. He couldn't understand the words being said, except for 'Ho'. He recognized the sound of that. It was his. The pasty-faced woman must not take it. Ho opened his mouth. He screamed like a pot-bellied pig being hunted through the rainforest.

'What's that dreadful caterwauling all about?' The volunteer gave him a slap across the head. 'Worse than a sick tomcat. If you go on making that sort of a racket, nobody'll *ever* want you!'

And for a long time, nobody did.

The sky was low, the climate remained cool. For days on end, nothing happened except, from time to time, a change of faces.

There was never a shortage of volunteers.

When one helper got worn out, or lost patience, another always turned up. It was due to Dingo. Although he'd lost all interest in war babies and gone off to record bear-dancing in Eastern Europe, his photographs spoke louder than columns of words. They inspired compassion in all who saw them. People felt they had to do something to help the scraps of life they saw in the newspapers. Retired post-mistresses, members of the Townswomen's Guild, schoolgirls

33

waiting for their A-level results, all types and ages came to lend a hand for an hour or two.

And they meant well enough. But it was going to take more than good intentions to restore these children to humanity.

Ho was not the only one who screamed. Rage and terror was inside all of them. Some were biters too, like rabid dogs. Some scratched. Some banged their heads against the walls. Some sat staring and rocking from side to side all day long.

'They just set each other off with their bad behaviour,' said one of the latest volunteers. 'I think we should separate them, the good from the bad.'

'The bad from the worse, more like,' said another volunteer.

So the five wildest children, re-named The Unmanageables, were carried up to the attic. Each was put in a separate room, with a mattress on the floor. There was nothing else that they could hurt themselves with. The floors were spread with old newspaper. It was easy to change, like cleaning out rabbit hutches. Food was taken up in plastic dishes and left on the floor.

'They'll soon learn to feed themselves once they get hungry enough.'

With this sorting of good from bad, Ho struck lucky. He wasn't put away in the attic.

Amy

In her calm, dimly-lit attic room with the small dormer window, a patterned rug on the floor, a bed, a bookshelf, and not much more, she interrupted her grandmother.

'Granny, was that *you*?' she asked, afraid. 'Is that you who put the bad children in the attic?'

'No, dear. I'm not in the story yet.'

'I don't like what they're doing to the children. Why didn't you stop them? Why didn't you go and find Uncle Ho sooner, instead of leaving him there?'

'But we didn't know he was there.'

'You should have found out. I hope you get to him soon. I hope something nice happens to him soon.'

'Tomorrow. I'll tell you about Ho's first Christmas. Time to sleep now. Sweet dreams, Amy.'

The Kind-Hearted Widows

When Ho was one year old, he didn't have Christmas. When he was two he didn't have Christmas. Nor when he was three, or four, or five or six.

He didn't have Sundays either. Or Fridays. Or birthdays. Or holidays and schooldays. In the first orphanage, each day of each year had been the same as the day before it and as the day following. But now that he was about seven, or eight, not that his age mattered to anyone, least of all to himself, he got his first chance of his first Christmas.

For someone who knew nothing of celebration, it was a strange experience. It happened like this:

Four retired ladies lived further down the pleasant suburban road from Helmore House. They'd noticed the arrival of the children. Over the weeks, they'd observed the comings and goings and seen the bed-sheets, nappies, and items of children's clothing pegged out on the washing lines to dry.

Mrs Violet Higgins, Mrs Rose Smarting, Mrs Ivy Rowllens, and Mrs Heather McNabb, all widows, met weekly in one another's homes, to discuss these and other matters of local interest over coffee and cakes.

Some of the neighbours had begun to question how long the child refugees were intending to remain in the area.

'They're all Chinese orphans, you know,' said one.

'Really?' said another. 'I'd heard they were Siamese.'

'Pekinese,' corrected a third.

'No. The *Gazette* definitely said Vietnamese. I kept the cutting to send to my daughter in Australia. They've got a lot of them there too. They come by boat. They get washed up on the beaches.'

'Humph!' grumbled another who'd rather there were not any kind of -ese living in this dull but still pleasant neighbourhood. Brown-skinned, slant-eyed waifs and strays with all that laundry flapping on the line every day of the week, Sundays included, might lower the tone of the area.

Over the coffee and cakes with her three close friends, Mrs Rose Smarting felt it her duty to defend the incomers even though she'd never met them. 'They're not causing anyone any trouble, are they now?'

Mrs Ivy Rowllens, Mrs Violet Higgins, and Mrs Heather McNabb agreed that they weren't, not so far as anyone knew.

'It's not as though we'd object if they were to play outside once in a while,' said Mrs Rose Smarting. 'Would we?'

'Provided they weren't too unruly, and didn't break our windows with rowdy ball games,' said Mrs Ivy Rowllens.

Then Mrs Rose Smarting came up with an idea how they could counter the other neighbours' hostility.

'I've been thinking,' she said. 'I believe we should do something special for them. To make it clear they are welcome in our road.'

But not too welcome, thought Mrs Ivy Rowllens, who did not care for children. She had preferred the meetings in the days when they played golf rather than plotting charitable gestures.

Mrs Violet Higgins suggested that taking the orphaned children to the pantomime might make a good treat. But Mrs Heather McNabb revealed that she had already ventured into the hallway of the gloomy building on the pretext of collecting for the Royal Society for the Protection of Birds.

'And I discovered,' she said, 'that they are not like normal children!'

'We already *knew* that,' said Mrs Rose Smarting crisply, wishing she'd had the notion of popping round casually. 'They're little orphans.'

'They're *crippled*! That's why we haven't seen them outside.'

'Handicapped is the proper word,' Mrs Rose Smarting said tersely, even more annoyed that Mrs Heather McNabb knew so much more than her.

'Disabled,' corrected Mrs Violet Higgins. 'I had a niece like that.'

'So we'll have to think of something we can do for them that's indoors in the warm.'

That was how the ladies' Christmas project came about. The children of Helmore House were to be given the most perfect Christmas Day, one which they would never forget.

'We'll give them a traditional celebration, with all the trimmings,' said Mrs Rose Smarting.

'A tree, of course.'

'The biggest tree there's ever been. Up to the ceiling of their sitting room.'

'And we'll drape it with tinsel.'

'And decorate it with sparkly lights.'

'And coloured glass baubles.'

'And silver streamers, and glass bells, and a star on the top, and a Christmas fairy just underneath.'

'And there'll be a Christmas dinner. With turkey.'

'And sausages. And chestnut stuffing.'

'And presents, of course. Lots and lots of presents. The girls could have dolls. The boys could have teddies.'

'Though they may already have soft animals of their own,' interrupted Mrs Rose Smarting.

'I believe I spotted some quite *big* boys in there,' added Mrs Heather McNabb. 'Mightn't they be a little too old for teddies?'

'How about small construction kits? Most boys enjoy making things.'

Later that day, Mrs Rose Smarting felt a warm comforting glow inside as she wrote out lists of what needed to be done. It was so marvellous to be able to plan something for others less fortunate than herself.

The month was October. That still left enough time, just.

She looked up 'Helmore House' in the telephone book and rang them up. She was a little surprised, though hugely relieved, to discover that the people at Helmore House hadn't yet made any Christmas plans of their own.

She wasn't to know that the helpers rarely had time to give each child a cuddle or read a story, let alone worry about luxuries like parties. Getting two dozen children washed, dressed, carried downstairs (and some of the bigger boys were beginning to need two adults to lift them), settled on a chair, spoon-fed their porridge, then carried through to the Day Room, took several hours. By which time most of them needed changing again and it was time to start feeding them their midday meal. There were The Unmanageables up in the attic to be seen to too.

'So I asked the Matron there,' Mrs Rose Smarting explained to her friends, 'not to mention anything to the children beforehand. We want it to be a complete surprise, don't we?'

She wasn't to know that there *was* no Matron at Helmore House. The person she'd spoken to was just one of the casual helpers who turned up out of the goodness of her heart to scrub nappies and peel potatoes. No offers of help, even for one day only, were turned down.

In the first week of December, the ladies met to co-ordinate the plans. Mrs Rose Smarting had disappointing news.

'There's been a slight hitch. I've just realized that I myself won't be available on the 25th December. I've all my family coming over for the day, and I can't cancel.' She was hoping the other three might manage without her.

But Mrs Heather McNabb said, 'Me too. I didn't like to say so before, but I've my daughter and her boys down from Dundee for the week. I won't be free either.'

Mrs Violet Higgins, too, had arrangements for the 25th. Only Mrs Ivy Rowllens, who didn't much care for children, would be free. But she could hardly go along on her own.

'Not to worry,' said Mrs Rose Smarting brightly. 'We'll bring the treat forward to the 20th. That way *everyone* can be happy!'

So, on the morning of the 20th of December when the sky was low and yellow, four merry widows entered Helmore House in their Mother Christmas aprons. They wore jolly party hats. They sang 'God Rest You Merry Gentlemen' as they trooped across the hallway, passing the small wheelchairs, crutches, arm splints, and little Zimmer frames lined up against the wall.

'Oh dearie me,' whispered Mrs Rose Smarting. 'What a terrible odour!'

'Sssh. It's nothing to be alarmed about,' said Mrs Heather McNabb who'd met the smell before when she came collecting for the RSPB. It was the institutional smell of overcooked food and old wee-wee.

The inhabitants of the Helmore House Day Room weren't surprised by elderly strangers bursting in on a wintry morning. Strangers often appeared, then went away, never to be seen again. It was pointless trying to distinguish them. No sooner had you got to recognize the shape of a face, the soft lilt of a voice, the harsh touch of a hand, than that face, voice, hand stopped coming. So why make any effort?

As for Ho, on 20th December as on all days, he saw little beyond black death and red fire. His morning vision was always clouded with noisy night-dreams and dark destructions.

The ladies were confused. They'd planned to start in the Day Room with the opening of stockings. But the children wouldn't co-operate.

'Come on now, dearie! Unwrap it! Unwrap the little parcel inside your stocking!' Mrs Rose Smarting urged the little boy with the sprouting black hair.

Ho heard the nagging tone. 'Unwrap it! Unwrap it! Unwrap it!' But he wasn't in Santaland. He was still lost in warland. He tore at the paper, just as he tore at his eyes every morning, to pull away the night-sights. He ripped the paper into shreds, just as his companions all around were at their similar work of destruction, furiously tearing at coloured paper.

'Gently now, dearie,' said Mrs Rose Smarting. She tried to help the little boy retrieve a tiny toy from inside its bright wrapping. Shapes of blue plastic fell from the parcel.

Broken bits. Ho had often seen broken things before.

'It's a present for you. We must fix the pieces together and make the little jet which you can play with.'

Ho had seen jets before. They screamed through the sky bringing fire and noise and pain. He didn't want to hold one in his hand. He threw the jet at the old smiling face.

Mai Le, the girl next to him, had a doll pushed into her lap.

'Here you are, my dear. Your very own baby doll. To have and to hold for always!' said the old lady.

The girl stared at the stiff creature. Memories flickered. Long ago, there'd been a motionless baby like this, cradled in her mother's arms. When the flame-throwers burned down the house, the baby's skin had curled off like fruit peel.

Mai Le shook the plastic baby. It gave no sign of life. It was as dead as her baby sister.

'Aah. They're completely overcome. I dare say it reminds them of traditional celebrations from their own country,' said Mrs Violet Higgins, gazing fondly at the angry and stupefied children.

How was she to know that at the Hoi Duc Anh no festival had ever been celebrated. Not Tet New Year, not the Feast of the Hungry Spirits, nor any of the Catholic Saints' Days.

Ho made a grab for more of the bright crackly paper.

'No, dear. That one's not yours. You've had your present. Try not to be greedy, there's a good boy. Christmas is a time for sharing.'

'That's right, Violet. Even if they're foreigners, it's important they should learn our ways, isn't it?'

'Soon be dinner time,' said Mrs Rose Smarting hopefully.

At midday, the plastic bowls were piled high.

'Roast turkey, done to a turn,' said Mrs Rose Smarting proudly.

'Lovely little sausages,' said Mrs Violet Higgins.

'Bacon rolls,' said Mrs Ivy Rowllens.

'Sage and onion stuffing.'

'Brown gravy.'

'Roast potatoes.'

'Roast parsnips.'

'Brussel sprouts.'

And then, more food.

'Plum pudding.'

'With whipped cream.'

'Or ice-cream.'

'Or custard.'

'Mince pies to fill the gaps.'

Long before the terrified Brownies were due to arrive to sing their carols, several of the children were sick.

There weren't enough helpers to carry them from the table. They were sick where they sat.

'Time for Santa!' said Mrs Rose Smarting. 'Can we hear those sleigh bells tinkling?'

'Ho ho ho!' sang the milkman, striding into the Day Room disguised in a scarlet suit. 'Ho ho ho! Here comes Santa with his sackful of presents for children who've been extra good!'

Ho stared at the tall man with the cottonwool beard and the false laughter. He stared at the plastic sack, so like the black plastic bag from which the itchy woollen garments had been pulled when he arrived in this chilly place.

'And *are* there any good children round here?' chuckled the scary milkman. 'Ho ho ho!'

Ho recognized his name. Why did the man say his name? What did he want with it? If he took it, Ho would have nothing left.

When the man bent towards him, Ho opened his mouth and screamed.

'Why, dearie me! That's no way to behave on Christmas Day,' said Mrs Rose Smarting. But there was nothing she could say to stop the terrible roar.

'Here, Rose, let *me* have a go,' said Mrs Violet Higgins. 'I've quite a knack with tricky children.' But when she tried to comfort Ho, he bit her hard on the cheek.

One of the volunteers came over. 'He's a right little devil, is this one!' She gave Ho a quick slap. 'I'm afraid that's the only medicine that works with him.'

But it wasn't working that day. Ho screamed on. The helper picked him up by his arms, dragged him out of the Day Room and dumped him in the passage.

Eventually, he screamed himself into a stupor.

The milkman left. The four ladies started to clear up the mess of wrapping paper. One of the volunteers said,

'Well now, that's that. Better start getting this lot upstairs.'

'Upstairs?' said Mrs Rose Smarting. 'What for?'

'Baths and bed.'

'But, my dear, it's only just after four!' said Mrs Rose Smarting. 'Isn't it rather early to start putting them to bed? The Brownies haven't arrived to sing their carols. They're not due till five.'

The volunteer shrugged. She heaved a child into her arms. 'If you can suggest a better way, then go ahead. But every one of these down here, and the five kids up on the top floor, has to be undressed, washed in the tub, and got into bed before the night helpers arrive. If we don't start now, we won't be done before the Day of Judgement. We're not blooming miracle workers.'

'Very well, I'm sure you know what's best,' Mrs Rose Smarting sighed. 'I'd better give Brown Owl a call. I'll tell her not to bother with bringing the Brownies over. I hope they won't be too disappointed.'

By Christmas Day, the four widows had recovered from their charitable effort and each enjoyed a peaceful time amongst their own families and friends. At the end of January they were strong enough to meet up for a post-mortem.

'Nothing venture, nothing gain,' concluded Mrs Rose Smarting. 'It was a good thing to have tried.'

Mrs Heather McNabb agreed wholeheartedly. 'We offered out the hand of friendship to our eastern friends.'

'To the deserving poor,' nodded Mrs Violet Higgins.

'And we set a good example to others,' said Mrs Ivy Rowllens.

However, all four were disappointed to have received no word from Helmore House.

'A letter would've been nice, wouldn't it?' said Mrs Rose Smarting. 'A little thank-you card.'

'Or even a note.'

'*You* haven't received anything have you, Violet?'

'Not a peep.'

'Such a pity. It's important for young folk to learn how to show gratitude to their elders, isn't it?'

'Perhaps it's not the custom of their own country to express thanks?' said Mrs Heather McNabb.

Mrs Ivy Rowllens said nothing for she remembered that, as refugees, the children had no country they could call their own.

'Perhaps they just couldn't be *bothered*?' said Mrs Rose Smarting.

Mrs Rose Smarting sighed deeply. In her heart she was beginning to realize that the Helmore House neighbours weren't so much deserving little waifs as ungrateful and mannerless savages who should be returned to wherever they'd come from.

'Well now!' she said. 'No point crying over spilt milk. At least we're all agreed that generosity is important. So what shall we do to help our community next Christmas?'

'I believe,' said Mrs Heather McNabb, 'that we should concentrate on a cause that is closer to home.'

'Perhaps something with animals?'

'I've always been *very* fond of animals,' said Mrs Ivy Rowllens.

'There's the Donkey Rescue Centre,' said Mrs Heather McNabb. 'Crying out for support.'

'Donkeys!' said Mrs Violet Higgins.

'Now there's a novel idea!' said Mrs Rose Smarting.

'And linking so well with the Christmas theme,' agreed Mrs Ivy Rowllens.

So the four widows got going on plans to create a

wintertime treat for fifteen rescued donkeys. And the children of Helmore House got on in much the same way as before.

Meanwhile, in another faraway country another war had started which was creating new orphans. This year's victims of war were more newsworthy than last year's. Some of them got their pictures in the newspapers.

So passed another year.

How Ho Nearly Got Himself Mothered: The Tale of Teresa and Nurse Staple

Ho learned to feed himself with his hands, then with a spoon. But the blackness and the flames inside his head remained lodged there fast.

Volunteers came and went. One Monday, a new one turned up. She'd been a nurse. Now she was retired. She felt she had a few hours to spare, as she said to the volunteer who offered to show her round and explain what a volunteer might be expected to do.

Nurse Staple was shocked by what she saw at Helmore House.

'But this place is a disgrace! Children being treated worse than unwanted animals,' she said. 'For a start, the Day Room is so gloomy. Why don't you switch the lights on in there so they don't have to sit in the half-dark like that?'

'We've been told not to waste the electricity.'

'They don't need the lights on them anyway. Lots of them are blind. The rest can't do anything.'

'They're a whole lot calmer when the lights are off.'

'And another thing,' said Nurse Staple. 'Getting their names muddled up as though it didn't matter which one was which. And those poor creatures in the attic, how long have they been hidden away?'

'You mean the Unmanageables?'

'We mustn't move them.'

'It's for their own safety. And for the benefit of the downstairs children.'

'That's where they've always been.'

Nurse Staple stamped her foot angrily. 'Every little child is a precious gift from heaven and should be treated as such. Every child should *know* he is special. Each needs someone in their lives who loves them for themselves, by their own name, be it a mother, a father, a neighbour, or a steadfast friend.'

'We're only volunteers. We don't make up the rules.'

'We can't change the system.'

'It's up to the trustees. They make the decisions. Things have to be kept as they were at the beginning. In case the children get sent back to wherever they came from.'

Nurse Staple said, 'I don't care what some committee decided five years ago. I do know what is true throughout all eternity. A child needs to be loved if it is to thrive.'

She marched back up the stairs to the attic. The other volunteers followed, aghast, unsure what terrible act of vandalism she might be about to do.

'I thought I was coming here to help out. But now that I've seen what I've seen, I've changed my mind.'

She flung open the door of the first cubicle she came to. A child was lying on the newspapers on the floor. She was growling like a feral cat.

'If I can help even one child to know she is loved, then it'll be worth it.'

'They're ever so hard to love,' said one of the volunteers with feeling. 'It's because they don't understand nothing about nothing.'

47

'So be it. If one child gets to lead a human's life, that'll be a start,' said the retired nurse firmly. She bent down and with a faint creak of her old joints, she gathered up the child whose clothing was soiled, whose fingernails were long and cracked, whose hair was in tangled clumps with bald patches where she pulled it, whose arms were red with weals where she scratched herself. She was one of the most unmanageable of the Unmanageables. She was not a pretty sight.

'There, there, my love,' said Nurse Staple.

The girl let out a thin high wail of terror. She had once had a name, Kim Yen, though she didn't know it.

The old nurse made her way down the stairs with the mewing girl in her arms. 'It's all right, my love. You come along with your Auntie Pat and I'll take care of you,' she said to the girl as she took her out to her car. She laid her on the back seat and she drove her away to the house she shared with her elderly sister.

None of the helpers knew what the forthright retired nurse and her sister did with the wild screamer. They could only guess. Perhaps she bathed her gently, gave her a soft cot to sleep in, fed her mushy bananas and sweetened yogurt, crooned to her when she wailed, cradled her, stroked her hands.

Whatever it was, it seemed to do the girl good for, a few months later, the pair were seen out together, Kim Yen in a wheelchair, the old nurse pushing. Kim Yen was as limp and disabled as before. Yet there was now an air of peaceful calm about her blank gaze. She was not screaming. She was not tearing at her flesh. She was sitting, still and patient, propped upright with a cushion behind her. She had a patchwork rug round her legs.

When the old nurse paused under a big plane tree and pointed out a pigeon preening itself among the foliage, the girl's dull eyes followed the direction of the woman's finger.

The volunteer cook chanced to notice this small event. She was so surprised at the change in Kim Yen that she told her married daughter. The daughter said, 'Oh well, I might as well take one of them then, mightn't I? I've been meaning to see if I could help in some way now my own two are off at school. One more won't make much difference.'

The cook was uncertain. 'They're very difficult to handle,' she said. 'Don't blame me if it goes wrong.'

The cook's daughter went to Helmore House and looked at all the children lolling in the Day Room. They didn't seem quite as bad as the way her mother had described them. (But then, she hadn't seen the ones in the attic.) She chose a bright-eyed young lad who, though he couldn't speak, was able to understand and even to read a little.

Ho watched the boy being taken away. He didn't know where he'd gone. Nobody explained. Ho missed him. He watched the empty bed at the far end of the long dormitory. He thought deep fearful thoughts. The missing boy had been a night shrieker. Ho understood.

Shrieking.

Disappearing.

One followed the other. That's what had happened to the Unmanageables too. Make great noise. Disappear into nowhere.

Ho didn't want to shriek in case he too disappeared.

The helpers noticed this new silence.

'Just fancy that! A sign of improvement at long last,' said one who believed it was the slaps round the head that made the boy see sense.

'Looks like he's trying to get himself noticed for good behaviour.'

49

'Maybe he wants to be picked for fostering?'

'Fat chance.'

Now, there lived, a few miles distant from Helmore House, a teacher named Teresa. She liked her work. She'd always enjoyed the company of young children. She was an only child, of elderly parents, long buried. So she was, technically, an orphan, alone in the world.

As each new pupil arrived to join Teresa's class, she welcomed them like a friend. She loved them and remembered them even years later, though she knew not to love them *too* much for, after one year, they always moved up with their year group to the next classroom. She knew the maxim, 'Never become attached to any one pupil. You'll confuse the child. You'll upset yourself.'

Teresa, known as Miss Turner by her pupils, was kept so busy with each generation of girls and boys, and with helping out with N.P. (Netball Practice) and A.S.C. (the After-School Club) that she was left no time to settle down with a good man.

Her friend, who was teacher in the next class, said, 'You could get a dog.'

Teresa said, 'I don't care for dogs. I prefer people.'

'Not to worry, Teresa. You're still quite young-looking, considering.' Teresa was not yet old, only middling. 'I bet you could find a nice fellow to marry you.'

Teresa said, 'Maybe. If I could be bothered. But it's too late for me to have a baby of my own and that's what I always wanted.'

'A baby?' said her friend with a look of disgust. 'Personally, I've never really fancied babies. They're so demanding.'

'Not necessarily a baby,' said Teresa dreamily. 'Just any kind of child I could call my own for longer than a year. Never mind. I dare say I wasn't cut out to be a parent. I'm probably too bossy.'

'Why not adopt?' suggested her friend. 'You don't need a man about the house for that. And you can by-pass the untidy toddler-stage too.'

Teresa thought about it.

'There's this big house down the road from where I live,' said her friend temptingly. 'Cramful of kids.' She'd read about it in the local paper. There'd been a blurred photo of Kim Yen and her adoptive mother. Nurse Staple was launching an appeal for better wheelchairs for the Unmanageables so that they could be pushed outside the gloomy house into the gloomy grounds to benefit from a change of air. 'They've got so many of them in there, they're practically giving them away. I'm sure they'd let you have one, specially as you're a teacher, provided you weren't too fussy about what sort.'

Teresa's heart gave a lurch of excitement. She said, 'I'm not fussy. A child is a child. They all need love.'

And so it came about that one Saturday morning, Teresa found herself making her way towards Helmore House and standing outside the front-door. She was shaking from head to foot. She dared herself to ring the bell. When she did, nothing happened. She was about to hurry away when a volunteer, pegging up the washing, noticed her.

'Try the back door!' she called out. 'It's open!'

It felt like the hardest thing Teresa had ever done. I'm sure this is worse than giving birth in the normal way, she thought. She felt terrified of entering the prison-like institution. She tried to give herself encouragement. 'I'm a trained, experienced teacher. All week, Monday to Friday, I am in command of twenty-eight souls. I am strong. I am perfectly capable of entering this building.'

51

Once inside, she didn't like the stench, or the heavy fire-doors, or the sounds of crying all around her.

Bravely, Teresa groped her way down the gloomy corridor. She entered the Day Room. As quickly as she could, she chose herself the child sitting on the floor nearest the door, a gangly toothless boy. His name was apparently Ho. This struck Teresa as the strangest name she'd ever heard. But she knew she would quickly learn to love his name, and everything about him.

Ho was alarmed when the stranger with the pretty fluffy hair, the tired eyes, and the laughing voice took him home in her car.

'It's just for the weekend, Ho, to start with,' she said. 'While we get to know each other. I don't think we should rush it, do you? We really want it to work, don't we?'

Ho didn't understand the words. But after a while he grew used to sitting in her car and watching other cars and seeing traffic lights change colour. And when they reached her cosy little home, he allowed himself to sit on her lap though he had never done such a thing before.

'And you shall come over next weekend. And the weekend after,' said Teresa. 'For ever and ever. For the time being you better call me Auntie Teresa. But maybe, eventually, you'll get to feel that you can call me your mum.'

Ho stared. He didn't understand the words.

'Oh I do hope so,' said Teresa and she put her arms round him and hugged, just a little too tight. Ho pulled away.

'Sorry, Ho. Silly of me. I mustn't overwhelm you. But I feel I'm beginning to love you so much already.'

That night, dreams sucked Ho back down into the

familiar furnace of warfare. He screamed in his sleep. Teresa leaped from her bed. She rushed to his bedside. She tried to comfort him.

'What is it, my dear? What frightened you? Is it the curtains? Are they too dark? We'll get some new ones. You shall choose them yourself.'

She knew nothing of the past lurking inside Ho's head. Nobody had told her. Nor could Ho tell it.

She thought to herself, Looking after this lad is going to be a full-time job. If I'm very lucky, he might one day come to love me. But it's going to take a long time. Whatever, I'll do the best for him I can.

Every Friday after work, Teresa brought Ho back to her home. Gradually she accustomed him to her quiet serious way of doing things in readiness for his permanent move.

Then came a Friday when she arrived at Helmore House earlier than usual. She went into the Day Room. She took Ho on her lap. She said, 'Ho, I'm really disappointed about this. But you won't be able to come and stay with me this weekend. I've got to go into hospital for a few days.' She buried her face in his dark glossy hair. 'But I'll come and see you as soon as I'm out. It's just for a couple of days. Some tests.'

Ho didn't know what a hospital was. He didn't know what tests were. He couldn't tell the time. He didn't know the names of the days of the week. He didn't know that he waited for eleven weeks for the return of the lovely lady.

A taxi drew up outside Helmore House. Ho, waiting in the hallway as he did every afternoon, could see her sitting in the back. Her eyes were closed. Her mouth wasn't smiling. She didn't look so pretty. She was wearing a scarf over her head. She had no more fluffy hair.

53

The taxi driver helped her out. She walked slowly and bent over like one of the children on a walking frame. Ho stared. She looked different. She was different.

'Hello, Ho. I've gone as bald as an egg. But don't be afraid. I'm still me.' She gave a giggle which made her lose her balance. She put out her hand to the wall for support. 'That's what the scarf's all about.'

The head-covering didn't fool anybody. Ho could see under it. He could see the smooth bare skin of her skull. It was like an ivory egg. But not quite like an egg for some wisps of Teresa's hair remained attached, like bird feathers.

Ho remembered the girl from the attic. Kim Yen used to tear at her hair and pulled it out in clumps. Had this person been doing the same thing?

Teresa sat down, worn out, on the bench in the hallway. She couldn't even make it as far as the Day Room. Ho couldn't sit on her lap as he had before. She was not strong enough. Her legs were too thin. She put an arm out to him.

'Ho, I have to tell you something. This is my last visit.'

Ho couldn't keep his eyes off the wispy egg-head.

'You remember how I said I was going to adopt you, so you could live with me always, until you grew up into a man? I have been too presumptuous. It's not destined to be that way. It was God's will that I found you. It is now God's will that I cannot keep you. I'm going away. I shan't be able to come back.'

I'm dying, she might have said for that was what the specialist had told her. And if she had told Ho, it was one of the few things that Ho might have understood, for he'd seen many people dying—old men from the sheer weariness of war, babies from hunger, soldiers from their wounds, women stepping onto land-mines planted in the ground.

But Teresa could not bring herself to speak the dying word aloud. She could not tell Ho how it was too late for the treatment to work. All it had done was make her hair fall out. If only she'd gone to see the doctor sooner.

'I pray that our Lord will send another woman to love you. I pray He won't keep you waiting.'

She kissed the top of Ho's head. She said, 'Goodbye, Ho. Bless, bless.'

Ho knew what a sad face and goodbye meant.

She handed him a toy tractor in a box.

'For you. A present.'

One of the other children came crawling down the corridor and made a grab for the present. Ho didn't care. He didn't want a tractor. He wanted a woman with a head like an egg to come and see him and take him to her home.

Teresa never came again though Ho waited at the window, hour after hour. She was ill. She died. But no one told Ho. He trotted down the corridor and sat in the hallway watching out for her to turn up. She never came.

But the screaming did. In the night. In the day. When it was sunny. When it was raining. On days when there was mashed potato. On days when there were greasy chips.

There was never rice, never fishy-flavoured *nuoc nam*. But, by now, would it have made a jot of difference to Ho's well-being?

For orphans and victims, there's no equal share-out of the good fortune. It's win some, lose some. Lucky Kim Yen won Nurse Staple and a placid future, bird-watching. Unlucky Ho won nothing.

In the darkness behind his eyes, he began finding new horrors, worse even than the ones already there.

Amy

It was storytime. But Amy wasn't sure she wanted to hear any more of her grandmother's terrible night-time tales. Her grandmother began closing the curtains across the dormer window against the dangers of the frosty night.

'Don't want you catching a chill, do we now?' she said to Amy.

Amy realized that chilblains and a sore throat were the only painful things she'd ever had to suffer. She climbed into her bed (which was pre-warmed by a hotty in a knitted cover).

'Granny,' she said wearily. 'I'm afraid your stories are getting a bit too miserable for me. Couldn't you tell me a happy story about how you found Ho at the children's home and how you brought him back here and it was all nice and fun?'

'Amy, my dear,' replied her grandmother. 'It was you who asked to hear the stories about Uncle Ho.'

'Yes I know. But why did you have to keep telling him such sad stories with everything always going wrong for him?'

'Because they were the truth, or some of the truth as far as we knew it,' said her grandmother. 'Isn't it better for children to learn the truth about themselves than to live in the ignorant darkness of knowing nothing at all?'

Amy said, 'If *I* got abandoned and then adopted, I'd

want to hear billions of really happy stories, about how I was actually the daughter of a pop-star or a princess.'

'Would you? I wonder.'

'Definitely.'

Her grandmother said, 'Very well, dear. I'll tell you a story which has an entirely satisfactory conclusion for it ends with Ho sitting downstairs in the big armchair, snoozing in front of the fire with a mug of cocoa.'

Amy said, 'You shouldn't tell the ending of a story first or there's no surprise. And anyway, Uncle Ho sitting downstairs is exactly what he is doing right now.'

'Precisely. And isn't that the happiest ending there could possibly be?'

Amy agreed that it was though she was growing suspicious about her grandmother's telling of the past. Uncle Ho hadn't been placidly sitting there in the armchair for twenty years. Amy herself *knew* he couldn't have. For instance, only the other day, there was that upsetting turn on the garden path which she'd *seen* with her own eyes. And a grown man howling was not something a girl quickly forgets. In fact, it was such a weird thing to happen that she was beginning to wonder if she'd imagined it.

'Snuggle down, Amy, then I can begin,' said her grandmother firmly.

Reluctantly, Amy lay down. She put on her resigned I'll-listen-if-I-have-to-even-though-I-don't-always-believe-it expression.

'Once upon a time,' her grandmother began, 'about thirty years ago, when it was round about bathtime, a boy with jet black hair and eyes as dark as ripe mulberries was standing in the bathroom on the fluffy blue bathmat with the pattern of starfish and sailing boats while the bath was filling up with warm water.'

Amy recognized the sound of that bathmat, though

these days the bathmat was no longer fluffy and the starfish had faded. She said, 'Was it *this* bathroom, in *this* house? With the bathmat that's still there?'

'Indeed it was,' said her grandmother. 'Shall I go on?'

'Yes please.'

'The boy was naked and very grubby.'

Amy said, 'Was that because he was so poor?'

'No. It was because he'd been out in the garden with one of his new brothers. And boys like getting dirty when they play.'

'So do girls.'

'Exactly.'

'Why hadn't he got any clothes on?'

'Because his mum had undressed him.'

'Why couldn't he undress himself?'

'There were lots of things he couldn't do.'

'Why not?'

'Nobody knew. They just had to be patient. He took a long time learning. And then he forgot what he'd learned. D'you want me to go on?'

'Yes.'

'So then the mum put some of the green bubble stuff in the water.'

Amy said, 'That was you, wasn't it, Granny? You were the mum then.'

'Yes,' said her grandmother. 'The mum was me. Only I call her "she" because this is a story. And she put the toy boats into the bath. And then the boy's younger brother—'

'Was it Ben, Uncle Ben?'

'Yes, it was. Ben climbed in with one of his favourite toys. It was a blue plastic jet he'd found inside a cereal packet. But quite suddenly, Ho didn't want to get into the bath.

' "This is odd," said their mum. Most days he

loved having a bath because he could splash and shout. But that day, instead, he started to scream. It was scary.

' "What's the matter, Ho?" asked his mum.

'Ho couldn't answer. He stood on the bathmat and screamed like an air-raid siren. The mum was worried. He hadn't lived with them long. He'd never made this sort of noise before. She thought the neighbours would complain. Or they might think she was hurting the new boy and call the Child Protection Agency. She slammed shut the bathroom window so the neighbours wouldn't hear.'

'Granny,' Amy interrupted. 'Why do you always have to make him be screaming?'

'Because that's what he did,' said her grandmother.

'Why?'

'Nobody knew. It took a long time to find out anything about his life and even now we don't know much about what happened to him.'

'Wasn't he *ever* happy when he was young?'

'On the surface, he smiled and laughed. But you felt that deep inside, he was in despair about something, if only we knew what. Some days, the unhappiness was stronger than him. Then it burst out like an explosion, even when he didn't want it to.

'That day, in the bathroom, the mum thought the little boy might've been screaming because Ben got into the bath first. Or he might've been thinking that their mum loved Ben more than him. Or that she loved the other children in the family better than him. Or it might've been something quite different altogether. He was yelling, "Not want not want not want!" Perhaps he meant, You don't want me. Perhaps he meant, I don't want to be here. Or perhaps he meant he didn't want green bubbles in the water because he'd never had them before. It didn't occur to her that he was screaming because he didn't like the way Ben kept making the plastic jet sploosh through the foam because it reminded him of bad things inside his head.

'Instead of making him get into the bath, the mum started to tell a story in a very soft voice. She wanted to let the boy know that he was going to be loved just as much as the children she already had, even if it was in a different way.'

Amy said, 'Perhaps the mum and dad, you and Grandad, were going to love him even *more* than the others because he needed it more?'

'Perhaps they were,' said her grandmother thoughtfully. 'Though I don't think so. As far as I remember, those parents didn't have favourites.'

'Why not?' said Amy who had always hoped that she was her grandmother's favourite.

'Because each child is quite different so there's no point in comparing them to find the best. A child is loved, or not loved, for himself or herself. And that's why I love you, Amy, because you are you and there's nobody else that I know who is quite like you.'

Amy wriggled contentedly under the quilt. She felt warm and good. She didn't mind not being the favourite grandchild if she was loved so perfectly. 'Could you get on with the story please, Granny?' she said.

The Tale of the Herberts

Once upon a time, there lived a happy, straightforward family in a small happy house. There was a mum and a dad, called Tim and Bel, and three children, a big girl, and then a middling boy, and then another boy who was a lot smaller. Sometimes, when they were going off on a picnic or bouncing on a hay-rick, or baking butterfly cakes, or even doing quite ordinary everyday things like having supper or learning to read, they wished they were a slightly larger family.

'It seems a pity,' said Tim, the dad, 'that there isn't one more person here to enjoy this.'

'It'd make us more of a family, wouldn't it?' said Josie, the daughter. 'If we had another person to join in.'

The others either agreed, or didn't seem bothered one way or the other. Tim and Bel asked a friend who knew about children who needed families what they should do. A few weeks later, a visitor knocked at their door. Knock knock knocking. The middling boy, Jamie, opened it. A man asked if he could come in. He said his name was Daniel.

'I'm your child placement social worker for this region. And I've found the very person to complete your family. Such a sweet bonny little creature, with a ready smile, bright eyes, three teeth already. I know you'd like to have her straight away so she can start settling down and by the time she's grown up, she won't ever know she's lived anywhere different than with you.'

'Oh. Uhuh,' said Tim, the dad.

'Oh umm,' said Bel, the mum. 'We didn't really intend to have a *baby*. We've done with babies now. It was quite enough when Josie, and Jamie, and Ben were small. And that was some time ago.'

Ben, the youngest, who'd only just started school, said firmly, 'Urrgheerrgh! We *definitely* don't want a baby round here, thanks. Babies are sticky and yukky and urrgheerrgh.'

The mum said to the regional social worker, Daniel, 'Thank you for coming. We'll think about it. But on the whole, as you'll gather, we don't really think a small baby is right for us.'

Daniel drank a cup of tea with them, ate some spaghetti, made a few notes in a file, asked a few questions, then went away.

Two weeks later he returned, knock knock knocking at the door. This time, it was Mum who opened it. Daniel was smiling. He was looking so pleased with himself.

'I've found just the person you need to complete your family,' he said. 'The very one. Ooh, she's so sweet. Such a dear young miss. Mischievous as they come. With a cheeky grin. She's three and a half.'

'Urrgheerrgh!' said Ben. 'We don't want any toddlers round here.'

'That's because you've only just finished being a toddler yourself,' said his big sister, Josie.

'No it isn't. It's because they can't talk properly. They snatch your toys. They scream. They wet themselves. And they dribble!'

'Aha, yes,' said Daniel. 'The lad's right. I believe they do.'

The mum said, 'If Ben says he's not on for toddlers, then we none of us are. We've got to be in agreement on this. It's a family matter. Every one of us is involved. So we really need exactly the right person.'

'Yes, I quite understand,' said Daniel, though he didn't for he had no children of his own. Nor a wife. His comfort and support was his racing bike with twenty-three gears.

He went away. Some weeks later, he was back, knocking at the door, knock knocky knocketty. Dad opened up, invited him in to join them at the kitchen table where they'd just started their supper of casseroled chicken with carrots.

'Home cooking!' said Daniel. 'Smells marvellous. Thank you.' He looked as though he hadn't eaten since the last time he was here.

Mum wondered how it was that Daniel managed to turn up exactly at suppertime. Was it because he had no wife or children so he didn't understand about regular mealtimes?

'Fetch another plate for Daniel, will you, Jamie,' she said, for she knew that if you couldn't welcome a hungry social worker to share your stew, you'd hardly be able to welcome a familyless child to share your whole way of life.

Daniel said, 'I've found *just* the person for you! Well, actually it's not a person. It's two people. Twin sisters!'

'Two children?' said Mum. 'And how old are they?'

'Five. Five each that is, ten if you count both.'

'Ah,' said Dad. 'We weren't actually thinking of two children. Not unless we move to a larger house first. It's already a tight fit upstairs with the bunk beds.'

'Perhaps you could take one of them then, to be going on with?' Daniel suggested.

'Split twins up? Definitely not!' said Jamie. 'Sisters or brothers ought to stay together. If I hadn't got any family apart from Ben, I'd certainly want us to stick together. And so would he.'

'Never mind. I'm sure I'll find a family soon who's just longing for twins.' Daniel rummaged in his brief-case. He pulled out a file of photographs, a whole variety show of different children, short and tall, thin and chubby, smiling and solemn. 'Are you *quite* sure you don't want a baby? Most people do. I've another really cute little one here, just come in.'

Josie said, 'No thank you. Not a baby, not a toddler, not twins.'

So Daniel put away the photos. 'You can't pick and choose. It's not like shopping, you know!' he said tersely.

'It never is,' said Dad. 'Whatever way you make a family.'

Daniel went away in a huff. Josie, Jamie, and Ben thought that was probably the end of the matter. The right person for their family didn't exist. They got on with their busy lives, going to school, coming home from school, playing football, messing about in the garden, having Mum's birthday, having Ben's birthday.

Weeks passed. A long while after Daniel's last visit, a tall quiet woman with long flowery skirts called. She tapped so gently at the front door that they weren't even sure they'd heard anything.

Luckily, the quiet woman was persistent. She pushed open the door. She came softly in.

'Good evening,' she said to Tim, Bel, and their three children who were in their kitchen eating shepherd's pie with french beans and sweetcorn. 'I'm your new social worker. I have been informed that you are looking for just the right type of child to join your family.'

'That's right,' said Tim. 'But we've given up hope.'

'Yes. I've heard that you're unusually fussy. But this, in my opinion, is no bad thing since people who know what they are after, often show more lasting commitment to whatever it is. There is a child I have chosen as he is just right for you. He would not be right for any other family. Here is his photograph. And here is the address where he lives.'

As soon as she'd handed over the photograph of the child, she disappeared. They never saw her again.

The family gathered round to look at the photograph. They all agreed that the boy looked exactly right, not too fat, not too thin, not too short, not too tall. His merry eyes were twinkling in just the right way. His cheery smile was friendly. So they finished their shepherd's pie, and set out at once to the address they'd been given which was not far away. The boy met them on the doorstep of the children's home with outstretched arms, almost as though he was expecting them.

'Would you like to come and live with us as part of our family?' they asked.

'I would,' replied the boy eagerly.

'Then come home with us and we will love you and cherish you as our own son and brother.'

So they all went home and lived happily ever after.

The end.

Amy was Doubtful

She said, 'That's a lovely story, Granny, but are you *quite* sure that's how it happened?'

'In the story, yes,' said her grandmother. 'That's how it ends, happily and quickly. Because it's getting late and I must go and help Grandad and Uncle Ho with the washing up because they do drop things so.'

'But in true life?' Amy asked. 'What actually happened?'

'I've told you your story for today.'

'I don't believe it was really like that. It sounds too quick and easy. My mum told me it was very difficult for Uncle Ho, being adopted. And difficult for everybody. Grandad said so too.'

Her grandmother said, 'I thought you said you wanted a proper happy ending?'

Amy said, 'Not with this part. I know the happy ending with Uncle Ho downstairs. But I want the story to be true as well because you said the truth is better than happiness.'

'Very well,' said her grandmother. 'Maybe tomorrow you shall have another ending. Then you can choose which one you like best.'

Amy said, 'Not maybe tomorrow. You're always saying tomorrow. Tell me tonight! Tell me now!' And she came out from under the covers and jumped up and down.

Her grandmother said, 'Amy, are you a spoilt brat who won't do as she's told?'

'No.'

'Good. Because if you don't get back under the covers, there won't be any more stories, tomorrow or ever.'

'All right.'

'That's a good girl. Goodnight now, my dearest.'

Amy's grandmother bent down and kissed her forehead as tenderly as she had kissed her own children many years earlier.

Amy fell asleep and dreamed of fairy godmothers in long floating skirts and wished they could be true.

And so, the following evening, Amy's grandmother began the same story over again but this time she told it differently.

The Tale of the Herberts Re-told

Once upon a time, there was a child placement social worker, whose name was Laura and who wore long straight skirts. She went to pay a visit to a family called the Herberts. She knocked firmly on their door. When there was no answer she strode in and sat herself down at their kitchen table. They were finishing their supper. It was Friday. They were eating haddock and chips from the fish and chip van because both parents were fed up with cooking and clearing up meals all week for their three hungry children, Josie, Jamie, and Ben.

Laura said, 'There's a child I know of, not that I've met him, who urgently needs a placement. He may be right for you. He may not. I only know that he definitely needs a family, or somebody consistent, to love him, though it seems he is currently rather unlovable.'

She produced a black and white photograph from her briefcase. It was small and blurred. It showed a large gloomy building surrounded by dark gloomy bushes with some out-of-focus blobs lined up in a row on the front steps. When the Herberts peered closely they could just about make out that the blobs were boys and girls of varying sizes, some standing, some sitting, some leaning, some lying.

'This is Helmore House, where he is at the moment,' said Laura. 'And that's him there, second from the right. At least, I think it's him. Or it might be one of the others. If you do decide to take him, it'll be a case of pot luck.'

'Pot luck?' said Josie. 'What's that?'

'It means that since there's not much background information on this boy concerning his past, you'd have to accept him as he is. And hope he turns out all right. Or pray that he does if you happen to believe in prayer. Not that you can even trust God these days, with the state He's let the world get into. In this boy's case, we suspect he's already been through a lot of disruption and disappointment. As far as we can gather, which is not much, he hasn't had a good start. Now, do you have any questions you'd like to ask?'

Bel said, 'Was he with his natural parents before he came into care?'

Laura said sternly, 'Haven't I made myself clear? We don't know.'

Tim said, 'Well, how long has he lived at this place?'

'We don't know that either.'

'There must be records?'

'None that we can find.'

Josie said, 'Does *he* want to move to a family?'

Laura shook her head. 'It's hard to tell. According to my notes, he is currently going through a negative phase. Anyway, it's unlikely he understands the concept of "family".'

Jamie said, 'How old is he?' for it had suddenly occurred to him that if he was about to get a new brother younger than himself, he could turn out to be a bit of a pest (like Ben sometimes was, nicking his paintbox, messing up his books). But if he were about to get a new brother older than himself, he might boss him about like his sister Josie sometimes did (telling him when it was his turn to help wash up, or feed the cat). These were not valid reasons for *not* wanting a spare brother. But it was as well to be prepared for whatever was to come.

Laura glanced at her watch and said, 'I'm afraid we don't have that information.'

'Don't even know how old he is!' said Bel. 'That's perfectly absurd!'

'He has no papers. No birth certificate. No medical card. We don't know where let alone when this boy was born.'

'Can't you tell by looking at him?' said Bel. 'Any woman worth her salt can judge a child's age by looking at his teeth.'

Laura said, 'From looking at him, one can tell he has black hair, dark brown eyes, and a light brown complexion and that he is almost certainly of Asian ethnicity. As for looking at his teeth, he has none.'

Bel said impatiently, 'Then obviously he must be about seven, if his milk teeth have started to fall out.'

Laura said, 'We believe that his teeth have come out through malnutrition. We believe he may have been seriously under-nourished at some stage in his life. This may have affected his development in some way, or it may not. So he may well be seven, as you suggest, or he may be eight or nine or ten.'

69

Ben said, 'Or he might be about eighty like our grandpa? All Grandpa's teeth have fallen out.'

Laura ignored him. She said, 'If you're at all interested, and naturally I hope you are, you must go and look at him.'

'Very well,' said Tim uncertainly. 'I suppose we must.'

None of the others said anything. But they felt uneasy. How could someone possibly join your family when you knew nothing about them?

After Laura had left, Josie suddenly got up and ran after her.

'What's his name?' she called after her. But Laura was already in her car and driving away so she didn't hear. And perhaps she didn't even know.

The Herbert family never saw her again.

Tim said, 'It doesn't sound hopeful, does it?'

Bel replied, 'No, it most certainly doesn't.'

Josie, who'd suddenly found a renewed interest in the notion of three brothers being better than two, said, 'But at least it's worth a try, isn't it?'

Jamie, who had some very difficult Maths homework to do that weekend and needed an excuse to do it quickly or not do it at all, said, 'Yes.'

Ben didn't give an opinion because he'd raced outside and was climbing the old apple tree.

The following day, the Herberts got up early, packed some cheese and pickle sandwiches in a basket, piled into their old van and set out to find the place Laura had shown them in the photograph. They were in moderately good spirits, except for Ben who was feeling sick. He was always sick on car journeys, even short ones. This was an exceedingly long one.

'Nearly there, Ben,' said Bel, which was a lie. It turned out to be far further than Tim had calculated. He should have left the calculations to Jamie who was good at Maths even if he didn't like it.

Ben pulled his comfort rug over his head so he wouldn't have to watch the grey crash barriers speeding by.

They reached the large gloomy house as shown in the photograph though there was, of course, no line of children waiting outside. In fact, the place looked deserted. They scrambled out of the van. Ben was first. He ran to be sick behind a gloomy bush. Jamie went and rang the front-door bell.

They heard it jangling in the distance. But nobody came.

Josie rang it again. Still nothing.

Tim noticed a woman with a dog on a lead coming out of her driveway on the other side of the road. He sprinted over. He asked her if she knew if her neighbours might be in.

'That lot? The orphans?' the woman said. 'Of course they're in. They're always in. Something ought to be done about it. It's ghastly! Too ghastly for words.' And she went tottering off down the road with her little doggie.

Ben found a good tree to climb.

'This is brilliant!' he called when he was halfway up. 'I'm going for the top!' His sickness was cured.

Bel saw a woman pegging out washing on a line.

'I'm only one of the volunteers,' said the woman. 'Saturdays and Sundays. If you've come to check out one of the children you better go on in. Not much to choose from. Just the dregs. It's in through that way.' She nodded her head towards a side door. 'The front door's jammed.'

Tim, Bel, Jamie, and Josie found their way along some dark corridors to the Day Room where they saw children and teenagers sprawled on the floor.

'Oh, what a nice bright room!' said Bel in an extra cheerful voice. She was lying. It was a dark horrible room with a cold floor and torn curtains. There were some toys but they were broken. Nobody played with them.

'If you give them anything decent,' said the woman following them in with the washing basket, 'they only ruin it. So there's no point, is there?' She set down the basket and began sorting and folding the great mound of linen. 'Washing, washing, washing. I even dream about it.'

A television was on. Nobody watched it. Nobody could've listened to it either.

'The volume knob's broken,' said the woman.

Jamie glanced at the flickering black and white screen. He saw military helicopters landing in a forest clearing. He saw children and old women being lifted aboard. It was a news item about the war which was in some small country far away.

'What a dreary place,' Josie whispered.

Jamie nodded. 'Yup.'

'Hope the parents don't expect us to stay too long. Which one is it? Or d'you suppose we get to choose?'

Jamie shrugged. 'Hope not. Suppose we chose wrong?'

Josie said, 'Then we'd be stuck with the wrong person forever, wouldn't we?'

She saw a girl, about her own age, lying on the lino floor. She banged two pieces of broken plastic against another. Josie watched and she felt sick sadness inside her stomach. She thought of herself as a girl lying on the floor clashing plastic all day long. There were some picture books up on a high shelf. Josie fetched a chair and climbed up.

The volunteer said, 'We have to put them up there. They only tear them if they get hold of them.'

72

Josie couldn't remember a time when she hadn't had books, even when she was so young she tore them. She remembered being propped up in her pram with so many books round her that she could hardly see out. When pages got ripped by mistake (or on purpose) Bel mended them. She never made a fuss about it.

Josie thought, That's what my mum's always been, a mender of broken books. These children all look broken, Josie thought. So I suppose Mum'll want to fix them with sticky tape.

Josie chose a book from the shelf, climbed down and knelt beside the girl on the floor. She showed her the book. She said, 'Shall I read you a story?'

The girl made a strange screwed-up face, almost as though she'd had her tongue dipped in vinegar, then grabbed Josie's arm and jabbed the broken plastic at her. The sadness in Josie's stomach tightened like a knot.

The volunteer washer-woman was looking at a list pinned to the wall. She pointed out a boy who was standing in a corner under the window.

Bel looked, Tim looked. Jamie looked. Josie looked. Ben didn't look because he was outside, already three quarters of the way up the brilliant climbing tree.

Bel saw a scraggy bag-o-bones. She thought, What he needs is a proper mother to feed him up.

Tim saw a lonely lad with his shoes on the wrong feet and his jersey on inside-out. He thought, He needs a dad to give him self-respect.

Josie saw a skinny person with forlorn brown eyes. She thought, He needs a big sister to give him a cuddle and a tickle.

Jamie saw a mysterious boy with darting, distrustful eyes who looked frail on the outside, but was seething on the inside. (And Jamie knew about such things because he sometimes felt them too.)

Ben was way up at the top of the tree. He didn't see the boy at all. He saw green leaves and a pigeon on a branch preening itself.

'Hey, you!' said the washer-woman to the boy in the window. 'Come here and say hello to the visitors. They've come to see you.'

The boy stared at the Herberts as though he was looking at monkeys in the zoo. Josie wondered if he was going to stab them with a bit of plastic like the girl had. But luckily, he grinned and showed his big empty mouth with no proper teeth, just two blackened stumps and lots of bare gum.

'Ho!' he said. 'Ho, Ho, Ho.'

The family didn't understand what he meant.

Another boy pushed in front of him.

'Me!' he crowed, flapping his hands about. 'Me!'

The Herberts didn't understand much better.

The volunteer said, 'That one's Phuong. He's saying he wants you to choose him. But I don't advise it. They tried putting him in a family. It didn't work. It's too late for him. He's too damaged. Calm down now, Phuong,' she added to the boy. 'You don't want to have to go up in the attic, do you?'

To the other boy she said, 'Show them round, dearie. Show them where you sleep.'

But the boy stayed in the window staring out at the dark bushes. So the volunteer woman had to show them round herself, upstairs round the bleak dormitories, the cold institutional bathrooms, the huge industrial kitchens smelling of old cabbage and disinfectant.

Tim said, 'Obviously, we'll need to have a think. So we won't say anything right away. We'll give you a call first thing tomorrow.'

74

The volunteer shrugged. The Herberts said goodbye to the boy standing in the window bay. He didn't even turn round. The Herberts hurried out to their van.

'Well,' said Bel, as they drove home as fast as they could. 'What d'you think?'

Suddenly Josie began to cry. 'Horrible, horrible, horrible,' she sobbed.

Bel said soothingly, 'Poor little lad. He wasn't *that* bad, was he?'

'Not the boy,' sniffed Josie. 'Not any of them. The whole place. It's dreadful. How could anybody *bear* to live there?'

'When they've no say in the matter,' said Tim glumly. 'That's when. Or when they've no choice. I dare say it's one step better than living on the street in a damp cardboard box.'

'Don't be silly, Tim,' said Bel. 'Children never live on streets in boxes. That's only in fairy tales.'

Jamie said, 'How can we tell what he's going to be like? We don't know anything about him. He didn't speak a single word.'

Josie said, 'We shouldn't have left him there. We should have taken him home with us. We should've taken them all.'

Bel said, 'Don't talk nonsense, Josie. You know we couldn't.'

Ben didn't say what he thought about the boy because he'd started feeling travel-sick again. He curled up like a grub inside his rug. He just wanted the journey to be over, to be safe at home in his bunk-bed.

They stopped at a petrol filling station. Ben got out and was sick in a litter bin. Bel offered him a mint to suck while the rest of them ate their cheese and pickle sandwiches. Each of them (even Ben, feeling iller by the mile) knew how lucky they were to have a real home to go back to, and not to be a person without a family, without a past, without an age, without anything, having to live in a children's home.

Amy Wants More

'Goodness me! Look at the time. You should've been asleep ages ago.'

Amy said, 'You haven't finished the story yet.'

'Yes, I have.'

'Not properly.'

'Oh. And so they all lived happily ever after. The end. Better?'

'But you haven't said if the boy they saw *was* Uncle Ho. And if he *did* come and live with the family. And I don't know if that boy was the same as the one who turned into my dad's brother. You said it was Uncle Ho's favourite. I don't see why. It's just as bad as all the rest.'

'Ho liked hearing about his new brother being sick. When he wanted that story, he used to say, "Sick, sick, sick! Poor Ben!"'

'Why?'

Granny laughed. 'I don't know. He just did. There were so many many things we didn't know about his life.'

'But, Granny,' Amy said, 'if nobody knew anything about that little boy's life, how could you tell him the truth about it?'

Her grandmother didn't reply.

Amy said, 'You had to make it up, didn't you? They weren't the truth at all. They were just make-believe.'

'My dear, it was a long time ago. Things were different then. I think it's time for you to go to sleep.'

'All right. Goodnight, Granny.'

'Goodnight. Sleep tight.'

'I will. I always do.'

And this much was certainly true. Amy slept tight because she'd always known who she was. She'd always known that she was safe and loved.

However, she was beginning to wish that Uncle Ho could tell his stories himself. He'd be more likely to get them right. Still, she thought she might try asking Uncle Ben. He was quite a talker. And she was in luck. The very next day, towards the end of the afternoon, as Amy's grandmother was putting the kettle on to the range to boil for tea, she announced, 'Amy, dearie, I have to go out to the Parish Council Meeting tonight. And Grandad's got the Allotments Society. So for once, you must see yourself to bed. I'm sure you can do that, can't you?'

'Yes, OK,' said Amy. 'But what about the bedtime story?'

Her grandmother said, 'Well now, surely you could read to yourself? Or if Uncle Ben is home, he might read to you, if you ask nicely. And don't forget to clean your teeth, will you?'

'Yes, Granny,' said Amy and she thought that perhaps, instead of reading her a story, Uncle Ben might tell her one, about what really happened when he and Uncle Ho were young.

So the moment that her grandparents had pedalled off towards the village, Amy ate the supper that her grandmother had put out for her on the kitchen table. Then she quickly cleaned her teeth, quickly got herself ready for bed even though it wasn't bedtime yet and she went downstairs again.

Uncle Ben and Uncle Ho were sitting either side of

the crackling fire. Uncle Ben was drinking a glass of beer. So was Uncle Ho. Amy knew it was good when Uncle Ben came to stay. He looked like her dad, yet he was different at the same time. Uncle Ho, of course, didn't look like anybody in Amy's dad's family because of being adopted.

Amy said, 'Please, Uncle Ben, Granny said you'd very kindly tell me a bedtime story if I go straight up afterwards.'

'Hmmm. Did she now?' said Uncle Ben.

Uncle Ho said, 'Hmmm,' too.

Amy said, 'So will you?'

Uncle Ben said, 'Maybe. It depends what sort of story you're after.'

'The one about what it felt like to be you when Uncle Ho came.'

'Not sure about that. I'd have to ask Uncle Ho.'

Amy said, 'Only if you can remember it.'

Uncle Ben said, 'Of *course* I remember. I was nearly six.'

Uncle Ho hiccuped loudly. 'Good story, that,' he said in a deep growly voice. Then he took off his glasses, polished them on the sleeve of his jersey and stared at the fire. 'Long ago times. Very good story. Very long ago. Screaming, loadsa screaming! And loadsa sick! Funny old days.' He took another sip of his beer.

Uncle Ben said, 'So it's all right if I tell her? How I remember it?'

Uncle Ho didn't say Yes and didn't say No. He just went on gazing into the fire as though he could watch life pass through the leaping flames.

Ben Speaks Out: How Two Brothers Gained a Third

People sometimes say that the youngest child in a family

is always the spoiled one. It's not true. The youngest is sometimes the one who is most neglected. This can be quite a good thing. It means you can get on with your own life without being bothered by too much interference.

Then, last year, my mum and dad got a new brother for me. Not really just for me. He was for all the family. But I liked to pretend they'd chosen him specially for me.

One of the boys in my class, Gareth, said to me, 'Bad luck, Ben. Bet it's hard on you, suddenly getting another big brother to boss you about.'

He didn't understand. It was just ace-brill.

Everybody was extra nice to me, because of me being the youngest. Mum and Dad were even planning to get the bedrooms re-done. In the end, they didn't have time. There were so many other things they had to do to get ready to receive a new child.

If you get a newborn baby, people send you lots of stuff, shawls and toys and cards and pink and blue presents. I know about this because our last teacher had a baby and we all gave her baby stuff so that her new boy would have enough of the rattles and dummies and teddies and books to last him till he was grown-up.

But when you get an old-born child, people are different. They aren't so pleased. They are surprised and confused. They don't know what to do or say, let alone what to give.

So Mum and Dad had to get everything by themselves: a bed (with sides because he might fall out); a plastic undersheet because he wet the bed; placcy pants because he wet his pants; a toothbrush all of his own (so he wouldn't keep using mine); a bottle of green *Ship Ahoy* bath bubble stuff (for me, so I wouldn't feel left out).

As it turned out, having re-decorated walls was the last thing the new brother needed. We got new duvet covers with Superman in his red tights flying all over them instead. I thought they were to make up for not having repainted walls. But actually, as Jamie pointed out, it was because the new boy wet his bed. Mum and Dad needed loads more sheets and stuff to go in the washing machine.

It got announced at school, when he came, in our NewsDay Round-Up. I was so proud. I was grinning all round at everybody in Assembly.

Then it turned out there was nothing special about getting a brother. That term, loads of people got babies in their families.

I tried to tell Ricky that my new brother hadn't been born to my mum. It turned out that being adopted was no big deal either. Ricky, as well as two other people in the classroom, was adopted. Another boy called John, and the welfare assistant who comes in to help Lisa. Three out of thirty.

That's ten per cent, as our teacher Miss Hammond pointed out. Which made it seem almost as ordinary to be an adopted person as not.

The different things about having Ho as my new brother instead of Rick or John, didn't begin to show till after Ho had been with us for a week or two.

One of the neighbours, old Mrs Oake, warned my mum.

'The green-eyed monster!' I heard her say. 'You mark my words, Bel! You'll have to watch out for that Ben of yours. He's going to feel his nose right out of joint, specially with the way that new 'un takes all your attention.'

I had to ask Jamie what the green-eyed monster was.

'Jealousy,' Jamie told me. Jamie's clever. He knows things.

Silly old bag, that Mrs Oake. My nose stayed just where it should be. I really worshipped Ho from the moment Dad brought him home.

He was older than me. They didn't say it. I just knew it. And he was strange and different and familiar all at once.

The first day with us, we went down to the river to feed the ducks with old mouldy bread. Ho ate all his bread before we even got to the ducks. So I ate mine. I made my footsteps match his, to be as much like him as I could. He walked in a funny way, slippy-slurpy. His feet dragged along on the ground as though he'd only just learned to walk. Perhaps he had. I didn't know. I just needed to be like him. I made my feet go slippy-slurpy too. And then my knees. Jelly-legs, I called it.

'Ben! Walk properly, do,' Mum said.

She didn't say that to Ho.

'I am, Mum,' I said. 'I'm walking like Ho.'

'Don't tease him. I'm sure he can't help it.'

I thought, If I try hard enough, we might become twins, though we couldn't be identical. He's got thick black hair. I've got light brown frizz. I'd always fancied being a twin. Then Jamie and Josie couldn't gang up on me so easily.

Some things, I didn't copy. Like, he couldn't put his own shoes on, getting them on the right feet. He didn't know how to.

'How did you manage before?' I said. 'You know, with getting dressed and everything?'

He didn't answer.

Mum said, 'Don't go on at him, Ben. It's not important.'

'It *is* important.' When I first started school, I couldn't tie my own shoelaces. It was bad, having the teacher do them for me while everybody watched. I didn't want that to happen to the new brother.

I shared my toys with him. He didn't have anything of his own when he arrived, not even a toothbrush. They weren't only mine. Some were Jamie's that he didn't play with any more. Dad bought some new ones for Ho, even though it wasn't Christmas, or his birthday. He got him a tractor, a green car transporter, three saloon cars, a lorry.

Funny thing was, he didn't play with these new toys any more than he played with mine. He just looked at them, didn't even take them out of their little cardboard boxes until I did it for him because I couldn't bear the suspense. He squatted down and rocked himself from side to side like a pendulum inside a clock ticking away time.

Tick-tock. Tick-tock. Left-right. Right-left.

He was nodding his head round and round and making strange bird noises in his throat. Did it mean he was pleased with the toys or that he liked the feel of his head rotating and the world spinning?

'Look, Ho! I'm laying out a long road, with all your vehicles and all mine together,' I said. 'See. It's a motorway. The lorries here in the slow lane, then the bridge under the chair and the filling station, that place where you stop and get drinks. And be sick if you need to.'

This was the kind of playing Jamie and I sometimes did together when Jamie finished his homework in time.

I thought Ho would like it too. He didn't.

He watched. He didn't join in. Perhaps he thought it was too babyish.

83

'You can play too, Ho,' I said. 'You put your tractor on the road I made.'

I had to put the tractor right in his hand. But even then he didn't understand what to do with it.

I said, 'You're right. Tractors are prohibited on motorways. And horses. Anyway, I don't like real motorways. They make me sick.' I pretended to be sick. 'But playing them's OK. Now look, so many cars! There's a big jam. What's going on? Oh wow! it's a huge pile-up. Send for the ambulance. Nee-naarr! Nee-narr!' I made ambulance siren noises. 'Send for the police car! Quick, where's the police car! Eee-aarh! Ee-aarh!'

Ho froze. Looked at me, grimaced as though he'd bitten with his bare gums on a bit of grit, then turned away and stumbled over to stare out of the window at nothing. He was trembling from head to foot and making little rabbit noises.

End of game. Time for something else.

'Ho, help put our toys away,' I said. 'Come on. They're yours too.'

But he didn't. Or wouldn't. Or couldn't.

Zena's newborn baby brother that she told the class about in NewsDay was probably a heap more fun to play with than this person.

Next morning, I couldn't find any of our toy cars.

'Mum, did you tidy them away?'

But no. It was Ho. He'd crammed them into a cereal carton. Then he'd put them in the bin outside the back door. Not just his cars. Mine too. Chucking them out with the rubbish.

Couldn't be clearer, could it? He didn't like playing with me even when I shared my things.

I got upset. Mum tried to calm me down.

'It's probably not that at all. Probably something else. I expect he'll tell us soon.'

84

Another of the odd things. He didn't speak. He made grunts and gurgles and animal noises. And he knew his name. He chanted it over and over.

'Ho. Ho. Ho. Ho.'

But he didn't know how to speak, didn't know how to play, didn't even know how to put his shoes on his feet.

Where has he *been* all his life? What's he been *doing*? We didn't know. We didn't understand. But there was one special day when I first saw that his brain wasn't just a muddly empty box. It was cram-full of stuff, stuff that we didn't know about, not me or Jamie or Josie. Not even Mum and Dad knew it. I'll always remember that day. I called it, The Day of the Scabbards and the Spears.

The Story of the Day of the Scabbards and the Spears

'He needs to go to school,' said Dad. 'There's so much to catch up on.'

He should probably have gone into Year 5. But they put him in the class just above me. The teachers made allowances, because of him being new, when he couldn't do things.

In my class, we were starting a new project. We were always doing projects. You only had to ask a small question and Miss Hammond managed to turn it into a project.

'Please, Miss, can a man run faster than a cheetah?' Garth asked. And next thing, we're doing our project on Speed—locomotives, cheetahs and other wild creatures sprinting across the savannah, space rockets.

'What's the distance from Earth to Jupiter?' That was Rohan. Suddenly, we're doing The Universe and Beyond.

'What's the biggest dinosaur that ever lived?' Everybody groaned aloud. Willie was a right dumbo. We did dinosaurs ages ago.

The Castles project was the best ever. For us boys anyhow. Not all the girls were so keen. Miss Hammond helped us find out about siegecraft and chivalry, about rebellions and reprisals. We looked things up and copied things out. We drew pictures of mottes and ramparts, of inner baileys and outer baileys, of ranks of foot soldiers armed with spears, of magnificent medieval catapults that would have taken a team of twenty of the strongest men to drag to the field of battle.

I got really keen. Discovering about castles was way better than playing with toy cars on pretend motorways.

One Saturday, Jamie had a football match, and Josie was round at her friend's. So Mum took me and Ho to visit a real medieval castle.

To reach the ticket office, we had to walk over a real drawbridge across a moat filled with water, and then under the portcullis with its jagged spikes hanging dangerously over our heads. The ticket office was in one of the towers. The castle walls were so thick. The windows were just tiny slits.

'That was to keep the invaders out,' I explained to Mum.

I pointed out to her the oillets in case she didn't know. They're keyhole gunports through the thickness of the walls.

I raced about the great castle, up twisty stairs, along the crenellated parapets. Ho stayed with Mum. They followed more slowly.

I crouched down at one of the oillets and pretended to

be a gunner warding off an attack from an army of warlords. I sighted my imaginary gun through the narrow hole. I trained the muzzle on the bushes in the grounds below.

'Zap! Zap! Boom! Crack!' I made the sounds of gunfire.

It must have been brilliant fun in the olden days when you were under siege.

'So long as you were certain your side was going to win,' said Mum with a laugh.

In a dark panelled room in the Keep, I found the museum of historical weaponry. There was some knights' armour, shields, spears, a reproduction ballista, and a genuine cannon made of brass.

I called Mum and Ho to come and see.

Ho shuffled in, flippy-floppy. The moment he saw all the exhibits, he froze. Then he darted for the nearest doorway. But it was only a low archway which didn't go to the stairs. It led into the next roomful of armaments. It was a big collection of Tudor pikes, swords, and helmets. This time he went berserk. He began to howl, he raged, he flung himself all over the place. His legs gave way. He collapsed to the stone floor.

Mum came rushing in after us.

'Ben! What on earth have you done to him?' she said. As though it was me.

Ho went on screaming, and began to swing himself wildly round the room, bashing into things. Before Mum could catch hold of him, he darted back through the archway and away down the stairs. We could hear him roaring from far off. It was like a wild pig being chased deep into the forest. He wasn't using words that anybody could understand. But you knew something terrible was happening inside his head.

Other visitors were staring at us.

Mum caught up with him the other side of the drawbridge. He'd wet himself as well. We had to go straight home.

I didn't even get a chance to buy a souvenir postcard to stick in my project book like Mum promised I could.

That was only the beginning. Things had to get worse, a lot worse, before they could begin to get better.

Ho had many strange rages. Our dad called them 'Ho-Yells'. He was trying to make light of it. But they were violent. You had to put your fingers in your ears. Even Josie couldn't get through to him once he'd started. Usually she had a special way with him.

I was young. I thought they were exciting, like thunderstorms. You know it's on its way. There's the far-off rumbling and grumbling. You know you're going to be a bit scared. You're expecting it and looking forward to it. But when it comes it's so much more powerful that you're terrified.

It was the castle visit set it all off. He'd seemed so quiet up till then. But seeing all those weapons, and me being so pleased, must have turned a switch on inside his head. Or was it like a plug in his skull which had been taken out so that all the horrible things jammed inside his brain began gushing out?

Ho didn't have words to explain any of it. So he screamed and banged his head against the walls, against the floor, against the door.

There was a terrible one in the bathroom. Mum said she thought it was because he was frightened of the green bath bubbles she put in.

'That's daft, Mum!' Jamie said. 'Nobody's scared of bubbles!'

She said, 'Maybe he's never seen them before? He doesn't know what they are.'

I knew exactly what set him off that time. It was my blue plastic aeroplane. Mum thinks I got it out of the cereal packet. Actually, I found it outside school. It was in the gutter, lying in soggy leaves and rubbish. I noticed it in the morning. It was still there at Going-Home time. I knew nobody wanted it. So I picked it up.

I didn't tell Mum. She'd have said, 'That's not yours to keep, Ben. It belongs to someone else. You know you mustn't take things that belong to someone else.' She wouldn't have let me keep it. So it was best to say nothing.

I didn't know then that Ho had come out of the gutter. (That's the family story anyhow. She may have made it up.) She didn't put *him* back where he'd come from. It was very confusing. Telling fibs and keeping things that came out of gutters. You weren't supposed to do either. She'd done both.

Every time I played with this brilliant aeroplane, in bed when I made it zoom through the air to bomb Superman in his red tights on the duvet, and in the garden when it soared through the trees and landed in the compost heap, and in the bath when I made it crash-land through the foam, Ho went crazy.

Other things began to set him off. The milkman standing on the step on Saturday mornings, wanting to be paid. It was the uniform and cap that did it. The fire engine clanging in the distance. That time I tried to play motorways with him, it wasn't the game itself had upset him. It was one of the old toys at the bottom of the box. It had belonged to Dad's brother, years and years ago.

To Jamie and me it was just a toy tank. To Ho it was real and life-size. He could see the tiny plastic man inside. He was training the gun turret on him and was out to kill him.

Poor old Ho.

Amy by the Fireside

Uncle Ben stopped abruptly. Had he got to the end of his tale? Or had he run out of memories? In the grate a smouldering log slipped forward. He pushed it back with the poker and Uncle Ho woke up with a jolt.

'That's more or less how it was, wasn't it, Ho?' said Uncle Ben.

'Yup,' Uncle Ho grunted. 'Good story. Bad days. Long times ago. Finished now.'

'Funny thing is,' Uncle Ben suddenly decided to go on, 'I've *never* liked visiting medieval castles since that day. Peculiar idea of your grandmother's, to think of a castle as a place of entertainment for two young children! She should have known, like my Miss Hammond did, that castles are about killing and spearing and pouring boiling oil on your enemies' heads.' He chortled to himself and poured the last dregs of beer into Uncle Ho's glass.

Amy didn't think it was a chortling matter.

Uncle Ben said, 'I say, Amy, hadn't you better be trotting off to bed before your Granny and Grandad blame me for keeping you up late?'

Amy crept upstairs to bed and read a nice safe book about ponies. She went to sleep with the light on, just in case. By the time her grandmother was home, she was sleeping restlessly, dreaming that her parents had adopted a wild war brother for her.

Downstairs, the spark-guard was in front of the fire, and Ben and Ho were side by side on the sofa crunching their way through a whole packet of chocolate biscuits and watching a TV movie. It was a scene of domestic bliss, though as anybody who heard any of the family's tales knew, it hadn't always been like that. Jamie, Amy's dad, also had his memories of the past. His were clearer, angrier, and just as troubled.

The Ho-Yell: Jamie's Tale

Once upon a time, we were a normal happy family. There were the five of us, Mum and Dad, my sister and my kid brother.

Then the new boy arrived.

My kid brother, Ben, was great with him. Treated him just like an ordinary little boy, even though he wasn't. At first, the little lad seemed so quiet, so perfect (apart from his lousy teeth). He did everything Mum and Dad asked him to. Or he tried to. He wasn't too bright so we had to help him.

Dad and Mum were always trying to teach him to read. They thought being able to read was the key to the world. He hardly even knew what a book was. He'd squat on the floor with one resting open in front of him, looking so engrossed. But the book was upside down. He wasn't even looking at the pictures. He was tearing tiny strips off each page and stuffing them into his ears. Perhaps it was to block out the noises. Trouble was, the noises were inside his head. He was blocking them in.

I'd been right about those troubled eyes. There was something inside him he couldn't handle. It was seething to get out. He used to creep up behind me. If

I turned, he'd lunge towards me, fists up, eyes slanted and mean, as though to attack me. He made blood-curdling noises deep in his throat.

'Hey! No, Ho. Don't go hitting,' I said. 'That's just not on.'

So he'd back off and hit himself hard across the face.

'No! Not that either.' I tried to hold his hands down. 'Don't go hurting yourself either. That's no good.'

He'd break away from me and bang his head against the wall again and again like a battering ram.

Then the rages started. My kid brother said it was something to do with visiting a castle. I didn't believe him. How could it be?

He had one at school one morning. You could hear it echoing through the building. Even the window panes rattled.

'What in heaven's name was that?' said Mr Richard, my class teacher. 'Sounds like the Blitz all over again.'

I knew. I didn't say anything that would draw attention to myself. I got on with my Maths.

The noise escalated. Other teachers were coming out of their classrooms to see what was up. Eventually the school secretary came to fetch me from my class. They're not supposed to do that, to get brothers and sisters to help out.

'We didn't know what else to do,' said Miss Russell, the secretary, ringing her hands. 'We thought he'd calm down if he saw you.'

They'd got Ho out of his class and into the assembly hall which was empty. He was roaring and throwing himself about, as though there were wild demons inside him trying to escape.

'Does he do this at home?' Miss Russell asked me.

'Er. No, never,' I said which was not entirely true. He'd just begun doing it.

By the time Miss Russell had got hold of our mum at work, and she turned up, Ho was back in his classroom, good as gold.

I went back to my own classroom. Everybody stared as I walked to my place and sat down. I felt embarrassed about what had happened. At school you feel responsible for your younger brothers' behaviour, even when it's a new brother you haven't had for long.

Worse than embarrassment was sadness. I didn't know what Ho's pain was all about. So there was nothing I could do to make it better.

That felt bad. When you're a big brother, you're meant to be able to help the younger ones.

Later, at breaktime, I looked for him in the playground. I wanted to check he was OK. I found him playing by himself. The other kids in his class were wary. They sensed he was unreliable, like a barrel of gunpowder that would explode if you shook it.

I watched him. He was involved in some private fantasy game. He was fighting off invisible missiles.

Stones? Arrows? Bullets? Meteorites from outer space?

He kept putting his hand up to protect his head. Whatever was attacking him, he didn't retaliate by fighting back. At one point, he flung himself to the ground. He lay still. I thought he'd passed out. I was about to call the teacher on duty. But I realized he'd been shot. Like in a John Wayne film or in *The Terminator*. He struggled back to his feet and continued to protect himself against the attack which only he could see. Who's put these terrible things inside his head?

Up till then, I hadn't really had a care in the world, except getting my homework done in time. Now there was a dark shadow hanging over us all. It was Ho's past, his pre-life before he came to live with us.

'Hey, look at Jamie's brother!' one of my classmates yelled. 'He's weird!'

'Yeah, a nutter!' said another.

I wanted to agree. But I knew I mustn't. I was a big brother. I had to stick up for him.

'No he's not,' I said. 'He's perfectly normal.'

'Dad,' I said, that evening. 'We've got to find out about him. Somebody must know *something*.'

I believe that's where Mum's make-up stories all began. They didn't seem to help Ho much. But they gave the rest of us something to chew on.

Mum and Dad made it their business to find things out. When they weren't washing sheets, changing pants, stopping him bashing his brains out, or taking him up to the Dental Hospital, they were pestering people, looking things up in archives, trying to trace that Laura woman who'd first told us about Ho (only they never did find her). I got even less help from Dad with my homework because he was so busy doing his.

Every time he or Mum found out something, even if it wasn't about Ho, Mum told it as a new story.

'But, Mum,' I said, 'you don't know if that kid they found living on that rubbish dump was our Ho.'

She said, 'No, Jamie. But it might've been.'

Josie said, 'And you don't really know if that volunteer who talked about sorting children into the wanted and the unwanted was telling the truth.'

'No, but he might've been.'

I said, 'So they're not really true stories at all.'

Mum said, 'They're true enough in their way.'

I said, 'But not about *him*.'

'They might be. We don't know.'

Ben said, '*I* like them even if you don't. And so does Ho.'

Dad said, 'Listen, Jamie, Ho hasn't had anyone to help him make sense of his memories like you have. Everybody needs to know they have some sort of a past, even if it's made up.'

Mum said, 'And once a story's been started, you can begin to lay some foundations.'

So she went on telling her tales. And we went on listening. Maybe Ho listened too. You couldn't really tell.

Sometimes, I felt it was slightly annoying of him to have to go on doing so much yelling even though he's quite safe. I said, 'It's a bit of an insult to our family. We treat him nice. He goes on screaming.'

Mum said, 'He's not screaming at us. He's screaming at something he's seeing from the past. When someone has a truly terrible experience, their mind can't always make sense of it. So the images keep coming back, again and again. That might be what's happening to Ho.'

So I hadn't just got myself a new kid brother to cope with. I'd got all the war-zones from inside his head as well.

Sometimes I wondered how my other kid brother was coping. He seemed to be handling it so well.

The Resolution: An Extra Important Idea by Ben

Once upon a time, a boy called Jamie (who is my big brother) was moved up into secondary school, and I was moved up into the next class, and our brother Ho was moved off into the Special Annexe because he was considered a bit odd. He'd been in our family for about a year.

In the middle of supper, our sister Josie said to nobody in particular, 'It can't go on like this. So what are we going to *do*?'

Ho was having a Ho-Yell. It lasted an hour. Supper was going to be late and scrappy. Mum and Dad sorted him out. Me and Jamie managed to get some food ready. It wasn't very nice. Overcooked rice and cold tinned peas. But it didn't matter. We'd all given up feeling hungry.

Mum sat silent. She looked desperate and sad and hopeless and exhausted. Dad didn't answer either. He was hunched over his plate with his head down. He looked old and grizzled. They used to be good fun. These days, Mum never baked butterfly cakes and Dad never jumped off hay-ricks and they hardly ever looked at each other. Jamie told me in secret while we were cooking the rice, that he thought they might be going to divorce soon. My friend Justin's mum and dad did that. Justin wasn't very pleased.

Jamie snapped at Josie. '*I* don't know what to do. *They're* the grown-ups. It was *their* idea in the first place.'

Josie said, 'They could send him back.'

I knew Josie didn't mean it. She was saying it for effect.

Jamie shouted, 'Oh no we couldn't! You know we couldn't. Well, maybe *you* could. But I know *I* couldn't. That place he was in was horrible. It made you cry.'

Nobody had any other ideas so they all went on sitting and staring at the rice on their plates. It was a bit over-cooked.

I'm the youngest in the family. I've always been the youngest. They never asked me what I thought about anything.

'Oh, don't bother with Ben. He'll be outside somewhere climbing a tree.' That's what they usually said. As though being the youngest also made me useless.

But I suddenly knew that I had to say what I thought. We ought really to have asked Ho. But there was no point. He still couldn't talk properly. He was over in his favourite corner of the kitchen crouching down, quite quiet. He always went there after a Ho-Yell. He rocked himself from side to side till he felt better.

It was obvious to me what we had to do. I wasn't sure how to say it. I wasn't used to telling the family what to do. I took a big breath and said it anyhow.

'We got to love Ho and love him. And go on loving him till he gets better.'

Jamie said, 'And if he *doesn't* get better? I never heard of anyone getting better from what he's got.'

I said, 'Then we just got to go on loving him.' I remembered when he'd done poo everywhere and it was difficult for me to feel like loving him, or even liking him, or even looking at him. Dad had to come in and clear it up. So I added, 'And if we *can't* love him, then we just got to put up with him for as long as it takes. Or for ever and ever if necessary.'

They all gaped at me. At last, Mum nodded.

Then Dad. 'Well done, Ben,' he said.

I felt so proud. I felt like the eldest in the family for once, all of them round the table looking at me and nodding to show they agreed. I'd said the right thing.

Then Josie started to sniff. She cried quite a lot. That's because she was a teenager and a girl. She got up, came round the table. She put her arms round me and gave me a big sloppy hug. Then she went over to Ho and sat down beside him and put her arm very cautiously on his, gently, like touching a scared animal.

'Can you hear, Ho?' she said softly. 'What Ben just said? We're your family. And we're going to love you and love you and go on loving you. And if occasionally there's one of us who falls short, who doesn't love you so much, there'll always be another one of us who does. Because that's what families are like. And we'll do it like Ben says, for ever and ever, or as long as it takes. OK?'

Ho began clinking two toy cars together. It was hard to know how much he understood.

So the rest of us hugged each other some more. Then Mum cried a bit too and I sat on her knee which I hadn't done for ages. After that, we just got on with it.

Dad said, 'It's like we're setting out at the beginning of a long journey when we aren't sure if we'll ever reach the end.'

And so it was.

Amy

There were so many stories and memories of stories swirling around inside Amy's head that she couldn't tell any more which were the ones she'd been told, or who'd told them, and which were the ones she'd been inventing for herself.

And were any of them the same as the ones that had been told to Uncle Ho? And what would have happened if he'd been able to tell his own stories?

When the Screaming had to Stop:

Ho's story as he might have told it if he'd had the words

Once, there was a baby boy who became a child, and who would soon become a young man. All his life, he had been surrounded by fire and darkness. Wherever he looked, he saw the crying flames and the black destruction. It was inside him too, so even when he slept the flames burned as fiercely and the darkness was present.

Figures came into his flickering world like grey ghosts through the smoke. He saw the gaze of a despairing woman who rocked him in her arms, then put him down and left him. She dissolved into the past. Other women came. Then floated off. Some pushed their faces close to his. Mouths moved and opened. He felt the breath on

100

his cheek. He didn't hear the words they said. The crack of falling roof beams, the thunder of bombs, the drilling of gunfire, the shouts of frightened men, were always too loud.

Sometimes he watched a soldier's thigh eaten by maggots. The man was alive and wept. Sometimes he saw a baby lying in the dirt, its mouth full of dirt. Sometimes he saw women escaping down the smashed road, time after time, and running away towards the green trees. He saw children without faces. He saw tall men with weapons. He saw aircraft descending from the sky. He felt the up-wind of rotating blades. He saw the skull and bones painted on the door. Figures came and went. They never waited with him in the dark places.

Some days he could remember nothing, other days he remembered too much.

Then people stayed around him, the same people, always there. Through the black fire, he saw them, day after day, year after year, never dissolving. They fed him and spoke to him like all the others had. But they didn't hit him. Nothing hit him. He began to hear them.

'We're your family now,' they said. 'We'll always be here when you want us and even when you don't.'

He didn't understand the words but he understood the meaning behind them. Some of them grew up around him, just as he was growing up. The ones who were already grown-up, grew old around him.

One morning, the young man who had once been a baby and who was on the threshold of adulthood woke up in his bed. He lay still and looked at the familiar sloping ceiling. He felt strange. He had never felt like this before. He sat bolt upright, to check if he was alive.

He swung his legs cautiously over the side of the bed. He stumbled to the dormer window and drew open the curtain.

Sunlight streamed in.

Yes, he was alive. And the darkness had faded from behind his eyes. There was no scream stuck halfway down his throat.

He put out his hand and looked at it. Yes. It was still there. It looked broad and brown and firm. Over the years, it had been growing into a strong hand which could wield a spade in the Garden Training Centre.

'Good hand,' he said aloud. 'My hand. Still here.'

Then he looked down at his bare foot standing on the bedside mat.

'Good foot.'

And at his other foot. Yes. Two good feet. He scratched his head. All present and correct. No headache. No fuzzy black confusion.

It was strangely wonderful.

He shuffled to the bathroom and peered in the mirror. He saw dark almond eyes warily return his gaze. He saw a mass of black hair sprouting upwards like spiky bamboo shoots. Yes, that was him all right. He saw a broad strong brow and a big smiling mouth. Was that really him?

He flattened his wild springing hair with a dab of cold water. He went back to his bedroom and dressed himself carefully with the clothes he had put ready on the chair the night before. He smelled coffee. He smelled sizzling bacon.

He followed their trail down to the kitchen where the old woman stood at the stove in her woolly dressing gown.

'Lo, Muh,' he said. He meant, 'Hello Mum,' and she understood him then.

'Hello, Ho darling. Ready for breakfast?' she said, as she always did.

102

'Ye. An toe. Plee.'

She understood. He meant, 'And toast please.'

'Two plee.'

Two slices, he meant.

'An piggy. Two rash, plee.'

He meant, 'And bacon, two rashers'. For, all the while that he was being plagued by flames and fear, he had also been going to school, then to college. Every day, he had been learning things, to dress himself, to recognize his left from his right, to know that bacon comes from pigs, and bread comes from wheat and that shoes must go on the correct feet or it's hard to walk straight. He'd also been learning that these people were not going to let him down or disappear.

'We're your family,' they said. 'And we love you.'

And now he understood. It had taken a long time.

The old woman who was his mum gave the rashers frying in the pan a quick flip so they'd sizzle on the other side.

'Funny old night I had,' she said, yawning wide. 'Awake till nearly four.'

'Poor Muh,' said Ho.

'What on earth for?' said Ho's brother who was finishing off his homework before he had to dash for the school bus.

The toast leaped out of the toaster as jauntily as a jack-in-a-box. Ho's brother caught it in one hand.

'Worrying,' said their mum.

'What did you have to worry about?' asked Ho's brother, Ben.

'Worrying about Ho.'

'Nah,' said Ho. 'Stupid.'

'That's right. No need,' said Ben, eating a piece of Ho's toast right off his plate. 'Ho's doing brilliant, aren't you, Ho?'

'Ye,' said Ho. He spread his toast and poured himself a cup of tea without spilling a drop. He nodded. 'Good sneep. No drean,' he said.

'No *what*?' said Ben.

'No dreaning!' Ho repeated. 'You know, sneeping, sneeping, eye-peeps shut, sneepy all night. No drean.' He meant, no dreaming. Ben understood. 'Just sneep. Very good that sneeping.'

Their mum said, 'Why, that's it! *That's* what I must've been worrying about. I was waiting to get up for Ho, and then I didn't have to!'

Ben said, 'Oh, Mum!'

Ho said, 'Oh, Muh!' too.

Ben said, 'Sometimes you worry even when you don't need to!'

Their mum said, 'You're right. I should've been celebrating instead of worrying because Ho slept right through! Well done, Ho! That's really wonderful.' She gave him a hug.

No wonder Ho felt strange, sleeping peacefully all night long without a nightmare.

He felt like an angel. Light-footed and refreshed. He was ready to face the day, to face the world, to face the week, to face the rest of his life.

Ho finished his breakfast, shouted 'Bye-bye, liddle brud!' to his brother as Ben ran for the school bus. He helped his mum wash up. He fetched his big workman's sixteen-hole boots, put them on the right way round, made some cheese and pickle sandwiches, put them in his lunchbox, kissed his mum, and set out along the road for the Garden Training Centre where he dug beds when it was fine and made wooden bird houses when it was raining.

Ho had slept right through the night. Without screaming. Without dreaming. No panic. No darkness.

He thought to himself, I am me. I like me. There was no looking back, not now, nor ever.

If Ho had known how to whistle, he'd have been whistling. If he'd known how to sing, he'd have been singing. As it was, he was smiling all the way to the G.T.C.

'Lo, bird!' said Ho to the sparrows chirping in the hedge.

'Lo, flow!' said Ho to the dandelions glowing like gold in the grass.

'Lo, lady!' said Ho to the neighbour leaning on her gate, as he clomped past in his heavy boots.

'Morning, Ho,' replied Mrs Ricks, the neighbour. And to herself she said, 'What a splendid lad that boy has become. A credit to the village. He's a right little treasure these days.'

A Christmas Story

Once upon a time, not so long ago, on the day before the day before Christmas, a girl called Amy went to stay with her grandparents. School term was over. It was holiday time.

'I love getting ready for Christmas,' said the grandmother.

'So do I,' said Amy.

There was a lot to do because so many of the family were coming to stay. The weather was cold but bright. While Amy's grandfather chopped wood and stacked the logs in baskets for the fires, Amy and her grandmother went to the market square to choose a Christmas tree. After that, they went to pick some holly. The berries were glowing so red in the sun the whole bush looked as though it were on fire.

Later, Amy and her grandparents had to bake mince pies, and polish the candlesticks, and peel chestnuts and wrap presents for filling stockings so that everything would be ready in time.

Amy's grandfather went up into the loft and fetched down the large cardboard box marked *Xmas & Other Things* and Amy sorted them out on the kitchen table so that anything broken or dangerous or which had lost its sparkle could be thrown away. There were coloured glass baubles and strings of tinsel and tiny painted wooden toys.

At the bottom of the box, Amy found a small cardboard decoration, stuck with cotton wool and one black felt eye. The other had come unstuck. The cotton wool was thin in places.

'That poor tatty old snow-bear!' said Amy's grandmother. 'One of the children made it years ago. Probably time it went in the bin.'

'Oh no!' said Amy. 'Let's keep him. He's got a nice face. He just needs a bit of mending.'

Amy got some glue and some fresh cotton wool. She turned the snow-bear over to stick down the cotton wool. She saw a scrawly name written on the cardboard. *HO* it said.

When she'd mended it, Amy hung Uncle Ho's old snow-bear on the tree along with the other decorations.

On Christmas Eve, Amy's mum and dad, with Amy's little brother and Amy's newborn baby sister arrived. And then Uncle Ho got in from work early and went upstairs to have a bath. Next Uncle Ben arrived from the station with his new girlfriend and his girlfriend's little boy. And then Auntie Josie and her husband and her three children arrived, much later than expected because the roads weren't good.

The house was very full. But they had a wonderful

Christmas Eve, and a brilliant Christmas morning. Then some more people arrived, Mrs Ricks from down the road, and a fragile lady called Kim Yen, who came in a taxi with her mother. And a fantastic Christmas meal which was still going on at four o'clock in the afternoon which was normally tea-time.

When they'd eaten themselves to a standstill, Uncle Ben stood up and said in a loud voice, 'Three cheers for the cooks!'

They raised their glasses.

'Hip hip hooray!' everybody cheered and clinked glasses.

Cousin Tom who was a toddler in a highchair lifted his plastic beaker. 'Cheers!' he shouted, and went on saying it till everybody laughed. 'Cheers, cheers, cheers.'

When they'd quietened down, Uncle Ho pushed back his chair and slowly stood up.

'Speech!' he said.

'Oh good. Time for Ho's Christmas message,' whispered Aunt Josie. 'I thought he'd forgotten.'

'Don't be silly, Josie. He wouldn't forget,' whispered Uncle Ben.

There was some burping, more clattering of plates. At last they were quiet enough to listen.

Uncle Ho smiled round the table. 'Peace,' he said. 'And peace. And family. And peace be with you family and be love. And peace.'

Then he sat down and everybody cheered and clapped some more.

Then the meal was over and they played charades. And then Kim Yen and her mother's taxi turned up and took them away. And Mrs Ricks helped with the washing up and she went home.

Later that evening, Amy's parents, and Uncles Ben and Ho, and Uncle Ben's new girlfriend, and Aunt

Josie and her husband, went out to the pub in the village.

Amy and her grandparents stayed at home with all the grandchildren as well as Uncle Ben's new girlfriend's little boy. It was a lot of children to look after.

Amy's grandmother said, 'Well, it's only for one night of the year.'

But Amy helped. So did her grandfather. They managed to get everybody into pyjamas, give them their bottles if they needed bottles, teddies if they needed teddies, and put every child in its bed, or sleeping bag, or onto its mattress on the floor, or into its carry-cot or crib.

Then Amy's grandparents sat down on either side of the fire looking exhausted but content. Amy knew it was time for her to go up to bed too.

She kissed them both goodnight. Then she said, 'Last time I was here, Granny, at half-term, you told me some of the stories about when Uncle Ho was young. Are there any more?'

Her grandmother didn't think so. 'We got to the end,' she said.

'Are you sure? I don't remember you telling me the ending. What was it?'

'"And they all lived happily ever after. The End,"' said her grandmother.

'Oh,' said Amy, disappointed. 'Is that it? Aren't there any more?'

'There might be, dear,' said her grandmother. 'That's up to you.'

When Amy got into bed, she found her cousin Emily was still wide awake and tossing around.

'Ssh,' said Amy. 'Or you'll wake the others.'

'I can't get to sleep,' moaned Emily. 'Will you tell me a story?'

'Only if you promise to lie quietly and try to go to sleep afterwards,' said Amy.

'All right,' said Emily, lying down and putting her thumb in her mouth.

'Once upon a time, quite a long time ago,' Amy began, 'in a beautiful place not far from here, where apple trees blossomed in spring, and winter sunsets reddened the winter skies, there lived a man and a woman named Tim and Bel who had four children and quite a lot of wonderful grandchildren.'

Emily took her thumb out of her mouth for a moment. 'That's us, isn't it?'

'Yes.'

'Has it got a happy ending?'

'Of course. It's got Uncle Ho in it. So it's got one of the happiest endings in the world.'

'Oh good,' said Emily.

'D'you want me to go on?'

'Yes please.'

'All right then,' said Amy. And she told a brand-new story about her Uncle Ho which had never been told before.

Other books by Rachel Anderson

The War Orphan
ISBN 0 19 275095 X

*A helicopter appeared above the tree-tops of the forest.
'Attention, people of this village! You are surrounded by
Republic and allied forces. Stay where you are and await
instructions. Do not run away or you will be shot!'*

When Ha arrives as part of Simon's family, the nightmares
arrive, too. And as Simon tries to find out about Ha and his
past, he begins to uncover a war-story which is not the one he
wanted to hear. Is the story Simon hears in his head his own,
or does it belong to this child whom his parents now say is his
brother—Ha, the war orphan?

Once, Simon had thought he was in control of his life. But
as the story shifts its focus between himself and Ha, he grows
more and more uncertain of his own identity. He becomes
obsessed by the fascination, the horror, and the all-engulfing
reality of total war.

'A rare and truthful book.'
Books for Your Children

'Compelling reading! . . . A beautiful, thought-provoking
story, profoundly anti-war.'
ODEC: Books to Break Barriers

Paper Faces
ISBN 0 19 271614 X

Dot didn't want anything to change. She'd had enough of that. Change was unsettling. It meant brick dust and disorder. The war was over and she was afraid.

May, 1945. Dot ought to be happy, but she isn't. Everything is changing, she's being moved from one place to another, and nothing is the same any more. Dot has to learn to cope with death, illness, and the return of the father who is a stranger to her. She begins to discover that there are different ways of looking at historical events, different kinds of truth, and many ways of being afraid and being brave.

Paper Faces won the Guardian Children's Fiction Award in 1992.

'Rachel Anderson has written what is in one sense an historical novel, in another a profound study of self-discovery, and by any standards a rich and deeply moving story of childhood. . . The book is masterly in its control of narrative, but the reader is aware not of technical excellence but of understanding and tender, tough humour. This is a very fine book indeed.'

The Junior Bookshelf

The Doll's House
ISBN 0 19 271734 0

'Oh, wicked,' she sighed. It was a miniature house. She felt sure she'd seen it before. Then she realized it was one of those dream houses from inside her mind.

Becks, a rebellious young girl who won't go to school but dreams of her 'perfect house'; Patrick, a very ill teenager who has to stay in bed; Miss Amy Winters, an elderly spinster who looks back on her past and on a very special birthday present. Three very different people with something in common—the doll's house.

And then there are the dolls, who watch and wait but can never intervene.

'A thought provoking account of how three lives impinge . . . the really sensitive characterisations and strongly contrasted life styles grip and hold the attention.'
Spoken English

'This is an original novel which explores a number of quite difficult areas . . . I enjoyed it very much.'
School Librarian

The Scavenger's Tale
ISBN 0 19 275022 4

The taller Monitor placed her hand on my shoulder.
'You can't,' I squealed. 'My family's opted out.'
'Nobody opts out, pet. Every human being has the potential to
offer the gift of life to another. Now take it easy. Just a little
shot. A nice sedative.' She took the sterile wrapping off a
syringe-pak while the other held me . . .

It is 2015, after the great Conflagration, and London has
become a tourist sight for people from all over the world,
coming to visit the historic Heritage Centres. These are out of
bounds to people like Bedford and his sister Dee who live in
an Unapproved Temporary Dwelling and have to scavenge
from skips and bins just to stay alive.

Bedford begins to notice something odd about the tourists:
when they arrive in the city, they are desperately ill, but when
they leave they seem to have been miraculously cured. And
then the Dysfuncs start disappearing. It is only when a
stranger appears, terribly injured, that Bedford begins to put
two and two together . . .

'one of the most powerful novels I have read this year'
The Times Educational Supplement

'The most extraordinary aspect of this extraordinarily
powerful novel for older readers is in its depiction of people
with learning disabilities . . . Truly innovative and daring
writing.'
Books for Keeps